LOVE'S PROPHET

BOOK 3 OF THE FIRST STREET CHURCH
ROMANCES

MELISSA STORM

Editor: Megan Harris

Cover & Graphics Designer: Mallory Rock

Proofreader: Falcon Storm

This is a work of fiction. Names, characters, organizations, places, events, and incidents are either products of the author's imagination or are used fictitiously. Any resemblance to actual persons, living or dead, or actual events is purely coincidental.

Scripture taken from the New King James Version®. Copyright © 1982 by Thomas Nelson. Used by permission. All rights reserved.

Print Edition by:
Partridge & Pear Press
PO Box 72
Brighton, MI 48116

*To Aunt Cindy and Uncle Darryl, who taught me true
love always finds a way*

A FREE GIFT FOR YOU!

Thank you for picking up your copy of *Love's Prophet*. I so hope you love it! As a thank-you, I'd like to offer you a free gift. That's right, I've written a short story that's available exclusively to my newsletter subscribers. You'll receive the free story by e-mail as soon as you sign up at www.MelStorm.com/Gift. I hope you'll enjoy both stories. Happy reading!

PROLOGUE

Jennifer Elliot had always loved a good party. The grand reopening of Mabel's on Maple was a twofer, which made it all the more fun! A doubly special event needed a doubly special outfit, and she decided her old prom dress would fit the bill perfectly. When the long-neglected garment actually glided over her slightly enlarged hips and bottom and zipped all the way up in the back, well . . . that matter decided itself. She'd be wearing her sparkly high school dance attire to the party—and that was that.

Maisie's jaw dropped when her friend floated into the diner on a cloud of satin that evening. "Jennifer!" she whisper-yelled. "What are you wearing? Is that your homecoming dress?"

"Prom, actually." She winked devilishly to remind Maisie of all the trouble they'd gotten into that night. "And why shouldn't I wear it tonight, huh? It's been lonesome by itself in the back of my closet for the past seven years. Besides, remember all the fun we had last time I took this little beauty for a whirl?" Another wink. Check and mate.

"Okay, okay, you win. If you call that terrible crime of time-travel fashion a win." Maisie shook her head and laughed. She wore jeans and a camisole just like she always did, making them the most and least dressed up—respectively—at the entire affair.

Elise and Summer soon found them, both in flouncy sundresses, which were probably far more appropriate for the night's party. But, hey, Jennifer felt and looked good, so who cared?

An older—but not too much older—gentleman she didn't quite recognize scowled at her from near the cash register. Why did he look so familiar, and why was he so angry? She tossed him a smile and headed out to dance on the black-and-white-checked floor with her friends.

Partway through the night, Jeffrey climbed up onto the counter and made a grand speech declaring his love for Kristina Rose and similarly his appreciation for Mabel. Everyone clapped and cheered—

Jennifer perhaps the loudest of all. She even whooped and whistled because all around her friends' dreams were coming true.

This night really was taken straight off the page of a fairytale, and she had dressed the part perfectly in her princess gown. If only she'd remembered to wear a tiara, too. *Darn*, that would have been so much fun!

This enchanted night was so much like a storybook, in fact, that it even had a villain. That same scowling stranger was staring at her again. Frown lines marred his otherwise handsome features. *Looks don't mean anything if he isn't kind of heart,* Jennifer reminded herself. She smiled at the man again—turn the other cheek and all that—and honest to goodness, his frown deepened.

Well, Jennifer wasn't going to stand for that. She marched straight up to him, stopping just inches from where he stood, and thrust her hands on her hips. She was nearly a foot shorter than him, which meant she had to be extra strong with her words if she were going to get him to listen.

"*Excuse me!* Who do you think you are, coming to this lovely party and casting angry looks all around the room? Are you trying to ruin Mabel's big night? And Jeffrey's? And Kristina Rose's? Put on a smile or go take your pity party somewhere else."

The man began to chuckle, first softly, but soon a full-bellied laugh emerged from behind his speckled salt-and-pepper beard. "Well, it's good to see that some things never change."

That voice, that voice—she knew that voice!

"Liam?" she ventured. "Is that really you?"

"In the flesh and blood," he responded, but then immediately frowned again. "I mean, yes, it's me."

"What are you doing here?" she asked, dropping her voice to a much kinder tone and immediately raising her hand to stroke his arm in consolation. "I haven't seen you since . . ."

"Since the funeral," he admitted. "Yes, I know."

"Nobody has. Seen you, I mean. So what are you doing here now? And why did you . . . I mean, tonight . . . And you didn't—"

"Slow down or you may actually finish a thought," he said again with a chuckle. "You always were my favorite of Rebecca's friends. I think you were her favorite, too."

"That's really nice, Liam, but seriously, where have you been? And Molly Sue? She must be . . ." She counted out the years on her fingers, but before she could reach a total, he answered for her.

"She's seven now."

"Seven? My goodness. Time really does fly."

Liam pulled out his phone and brought up the home screen. He handed it to Jennifer to show her the missing-toothed smile of his little girl.

She felt a sharp twist of pain right in the stomach. "She looks so much like . . ."

"Like Rebecca, I know." He smiled sadly and put the phone back in his jeans pocket.

"You still haven't told me what you're doing here," she insisted.

"I had to come into town to take care of some business. While I was here, I figured I would grab a couple of to-go orders of Mabel's famous meatloaf, but when I arrived, the party had already started, and it felt rude to leave without paying my respects to the old girl."

"And your idea of paying your respects is to stand here and cast dirty looks at everyone?"

He frowned again, but this time looked sad rather than angry. "No, at least . . . not on purpose. Watching you all, I realized that Rebecc —never mind."

Jennifer's heart softened. Now she, too, wore a sad frown. "You still miss her so much, don't you?"

"It's like a piece of my heart was buried with her."

"Oh, Liam." Jennifer couldn't resist standing on her toes to wrap him in a tight hug. "I know you will never stop missing her, but please try to heal. Do it for Rebecca. Do it for Molly Sue."

He laughed, but the sound conveyed no joy. "Believe me, I'm trying."

"Well, whatever you're doing on your own doesn't seem to be enough. Please come to church. Bring Molly Sue. I bet she'll love being a part of my Sunday school class. And you—you can't just disappear from all of our lives forever. Come back. The people here love you and want to help. We've missed you. Not just Rebecca, but all of you."

"I've missed me, too."

"Then you'll come?"

"I can't make any promises, but I'll try." He shifted his weight uncomfortably from one foot to the other, then zipped up his jacket and shrugged. "It's, uh, getting pretty late. It was nice catching up with you, Jennifer."

"Fine, go, but don't be a stranger!" she called after him as the door opened, letting in a gust of cool night air.

Please, Lord. If there is a way you can use me to help, I'm ready.

She watched until his silhouette disappeared into the night's darkness. So Liam had returned, but why now? And would he be back again? This day was too much of a gift to be wasted on what ifs. If the Lord wanted to bring Liam back into her life, He would do just that.

She put on a smile and returned to her friends.

Only time would tell what tomorrow held.

Tonight, she would dance.

ONE

Saying Liam James lived in the tiny town of Sweet Grove, Texas, was quite a stretch. While technically true, he lived so far on the border of the township that it took him more than twenty minutes to drive into town. Tiny in population, sure. But acreage? Definitely not.

His wife, Rebecca, had grown up in the main part of town. Had died there, too. On the other hand, he had grown up in the much larger, much more vibrant city of Dallas. Though he'd happily moved his entire life when his pretty young bride had batted her eyelashes and said it might be nice to raise their as-of-yet unborn child in "the type of place where everybody knows everybody, for better or worse."

And so they lived in town for about a year while

their dream house was being built on the outskirts of town. Somewhere during that busy time, they'd had a daughter, Miss Molly Sue James. Rebecca quit her job as a middle school teacher and decided to stay home full-time, both to raise their child and to help Liam with the business as needed. He'd slaved day and night growing his Internet consulting company from a one-man operation to a thriving corporation with a waiting list near a mile long.

He'd worked hard so she wouldn't have to. Liam loved Rebecca and wanted her to have everything . . .

And so everything is what she got, for better or for far, far worse. And that included cancer.

While all cancers were dastardly, Rebecca's was the worst of them all. Her illness took her mind before it took her body, meaning his final moments with her were filled with confusion, frustration, tears—for both of them, and especially their little girl who was six when her mother passed out of this world and through those pearly gates.

She'd started first grade less than a month prior to her parents pulling her out of classes and bringing her home. They didn't know how much time Rebecca would have left, and they wanted Molly Sue to be able to lap up every available moment, make every possible memory before it was too late.

So they homeschooled. Rebecca did the bulk of

the work, despite her illness making everything at least a dozen times more difficult. Molly never complained, even though one wouldn't expect a child to be so understanding of something an adult could hardly comprehend.

Liam would often find the two of them giggling under a pile of blankets while they took turns reading aloud from an old Berenstain Bears book. Molly took to reading like a duck to water. In no time at all, she and her mother shifted to reading the latest young adult fantasy novels. Rebecca patiently explained the words and concepts Molly Sue was still too young to understand on her own. And while the little girl's reading excelled, she quickly fell behind in other subjects. Science, especially.

By the time Rebecca's funeral had come and gone, Liam had already reached an important decision on the matter of his daughter's education. She'd need a private homeschool tutor for at least a year to help her catch up. The last thing he wanted to do was send her out among the other kids before she was ready. The social challenges of reintegrating his daughter into the school system would be more than enough without heaping academic challenges on top of them.

The one thing he couldn't bring himself to decide, though, was where he and Molly should build their lives now that they were no longer tied to Sweet

Grove. He could run his home business anywhere. Sometimes he'd go so far as to research Montessori schools in Maine or Wi-Fi speeds in Fiji, but he never made any serious moves toward relocating their lives . . . which meant they stayed for better or for worse, both comforted and haunted by the memories of the dearly departed Rebecca.

At first, his parents had gently suggested he move back to Dallas so they could help raise Molly Sue, then they'd nagged, and later pleaded, but still he remained firm. Somehow, he knew Rebecca's ghost would follow him to the far corners of the earth, so he might as well stay put in the dream house they'd built together, in the place where she'd wanted more than anything to see her daughter grow up.

What would Rebecca think of Molly Sue's latest artwork, that funny joke their daughter had told over grilled cheese sandwiches, the fact that he might like to repaint the walls to a sad shade of blue to match his constant mood?

He thought about all these things more than he cared to admit.

Sometimes he talked to her late at night when he was sure Molly Sue had gone to sleep, but she never answered back.

She was gone, gone, gone.

And yet here he remained, trying and—more

often than not—failing to be a good father to the daughter Rebecca hadn't wanted to leave behind. He was stuck, and he hated himself for that. But how could he make sure his daughter grew up happy when he'd practically forgotten the meaning of the word . . . let alone how it felt?

Jennifer Elliot woke up with a smile. She'd always been a morning person and didn't need an alarm to remind her when the time had come to rise and shine. Besides, today was her favorite day of the whole week: Sunday. Sundays were for God, for the children, and most of all, for really and truly living her best life.

She stretched her arms overhead, grabbed a drink from the half-full water bottle on her night-stand, and sprang out of bed, ready to take on the day.

"This is the day that the Lord has made . . ." she sang and then burst into a spirited humming rendi-tion of one of the songs she most liked to sing with her kids. Okay, so they weren't *her* kids, but then again, they kind of were. She loved being a daycare worker, but more than that, she loved being First Street Church's resident Sunday school teacher. She'd always been great with kids, even though she was nowhere near having any of her own.

She didn't even have a boyfriend, let alone any marriage prospects!

But with kids, what you saw . . . well, that's what you got. She admired their honesty, and above all, she loved the pure bliss on their little faces as she told them stories about Jesus and reminded them of the Golden Rule. Yes, her call to be a Sunday school teacher had come in loud and clear, and she'd happily answered. The only real problem was that it was a volunteer position.

Of course, Jennifer didn't care much about money. How could she when she barely had two nickels to rub together? Sure, it might be nice to have a bit more cash for pretty dresses, art supplies, and other things that made her happy—but, truth be told, she was perfectly happy already. Especially because today was a Sunday.

She pulled her favorite maxi dress over her head and frowned when she noticed a tiny hole had begun to tug at the neckline. *Oh well. It's had a good run.* Just to be safe, she pulled the dress back over her head and tossed it onto the bed, then went to make breakfast in nothing but her underwear, a pink polka-dotted bra and cotton briefs with a faded Superman logo across the bottom. No one ever saw what she wore beneath her endless stream of dresses, but knowing she had something pretty and fun beneath always gave her that added boost of confidence she craved.

She padded out to the kitchen and buttered some toast, carefully removing a chunk from the middle so she could make eggies in a basket. A train chugged by outside, shaking the floor beneath her. The track outside Sweet Grove didn't have too many trains pull through, but enough that she'd gotten used to the rattle and hum and, really, hardly noticed anymore.

Besides, you couldn't beat the price. Her rent was less than $400 per month, and she knew Kristina Rose paid almost twice that for her nicer place uptown. Nope, Jennifer didn't mind being poor. She had everything she needed. Besides, it's not like Jesus was rolling in dough back in His day. She giggled as she pictured Jesus in His long white robe and blue sash swimming in a pool of dollar bills.

If this life was good enough for her Lord and Savior, then it was good enough for her, too. Money wasn't what made people rich, anyway. Joy remained the only currency that mattered to Jennifer—having it, sharing it, spreading it all around like the generous helping of butter she heaped onto her toast. *Yum!*

She took her breakfast over to the small, messy desk on the other side of her studio apartment and booted up her computer. It was the one Maisie had used back when they were all in high school, which meant it was old—really old, like big, chunky box monitor old. But it had a working Internet connection and had been free, so even though it took its dear time booting up, Jennifer didn't mind too much.

She basically only used it for one thing, anyway. After logging into her Facebook account, she scrolled through her feed looking for updates from her family on the East Coast. She wished they hadn't moved away from Sweet Grove while she'd been away at college earning her education degree. Having to decide between the only home she'd ever known and the family she loved had been a terrible thing, one that had torn her up for months as she went back and forth, back and forth, weighing all the pros and cons.

Ultimately, the visit to Jessica's new home in Baltimore is what made the decision for her. Even though her sister, nieces, and parents had all relocated, Jennifer just couldn't picture herself making a life in such a large, impersonal town. Life moved too fast over there. She liked the pace Sweet Grove had set for her years ago and preferred not to live a life of rushing from one appointment to the next if she could avoid it.

So here she was, in her undies, working on her ancient computer, eating eggies in a basket. No news from her sister or mom. They didn't post too much anyway. Maybe Jennifer would give them a call after church. But first she had a hole to stitch, children to teach, and a song to sing . . .

"This is the day that the Lord has made. Let us rejoice and be glad in it!" she belted out as she finished her morning chores, poor as a church mouse but happy as a clam, which of course was another strange picture that made Jennifer giggle.

TWO

Sundays were the one day each week Liam allowed himself to sleep late. Most days he rose before the sun and shuffled over to his dark office to boot up his laptop and start work. On Sundays, he woke up slightly after dawn and cooked Mickey Mouse pancakes for himself and Molly Sue, a tradition his late wife had started and one he didn't see himself putting an end to anytime soon. He could just picture himself, withered and old, sitting in the nursing home with an oxygen tank at his side as he shook his fists and demanded Mickey Mouse pancakes with chocolate chips cooked right into the batter.

By then Molly would have her own children,

maybe even grandchildren, and Liam would still be alone—more alone.

He lifted the skillet and with a quick maneuver tossed the flapjack up and over . . . onto the side of the pan. He would never be as good at this as Rebecca had been, but he'd keep trying because it seemed like a nice way to honor her memory, even though he did a rather unremarkable job with this particular tribute.

He poured himself a glass of orange juice and briefly contemplated adding a splash of vodka before thinking better of it. He already felt as if he moved around in a haze and didn't need to further numb the remaining senses he had at his disposal. Besides, Molly would be down to join him in . . .

He glanced at the clock above the oven and realized Molly Sue was behind schedule that morning. Usually she sat on a bar stool across from where he worked at the kitchen island and recounted her dreams from the night before with vivid detail. It wasn't like her to sleep in, especially considering how much she loved their special Sunday morning ritual. Could she be coming down with something?

It was December, which meant peak cold season around these parts. Poor kid never got a snow day because she lived in Texas and never got a sick day because she was homeschooled. Maybe he could set her up with some movies and books in bed tomorrow, call off her tutor, give the girl a break.

Lord knew she needed one. Heck, so did he.

He finished making their pancakes, and the second one thankfully came out better than the first. That would be for Molly. He cut some strawberries, added some whipped cream, and prepared a breakfast tray to serve to Molly in bed. If she was feeling up to it, he'd go back down and grab his plate to join her. If not, he'd let her sleep and start work early for the day.

As he drew near Molly Sue's bedroom, he heard singing—the song from *Frozen* but not the one everyone had been obsessed with a couple of years back.

"Hi, Daddy!" She beamed at him, standing amid an alarming pile of rumpled, discarded clothes. She wore a sparkly tutu that he seemed to recall belonging to a Halloween costume from the year before, striped knee socks, and pretty much every piece of jewelry she owned, including a sapphire pendant her mother had left for her—a sapphire pendant Molly Sue was not supposed to wear without permission.

"Don't be upset, Daddy," she said with a smile followed by an inelegant twirl. "I needed to look nice today."

"You always look nice," he answered, crossing the room to leave the breakfast tray on her unmade bed.

She let out an exaggerated sigh complete with a giant heave of her shoulders. "Yes, but I had to look extra nice. Do I look *extra* nice?" She raised an eyebrow at him, a gesture she'd inherited from her mother, much like that pendant she wore.

"Yes, you look beautiful."

A smile bloomed across her face, and she spun again, then bowed. "Thank you, Daddy. Are those Mickey Mouse pancakes for me?" she asked pointing toward the bed.

"They sure are. Are you hungry?"

She brought a hand to her belly and frowned. "I am hungry, but we don't have much time."

"Time? Time for what?"

"We have to go, or we won't make it!" She frantically searched her nightstand and then pulled out her small digital clock and groaned.

"Hey, slow down already. What's wrong? Where are we going?"

She rolled her eyes at him. So much guff from a seven-year-old, and he didn't know why he was in trouble to begin with! "It's Sunday," she said, placing a hand on each hip. "You know what that means."

"Yes, it's Mickey Mouse pancake day." He smiled and raised the tray toward her as a peace offering, even though he still had no idea what they warring over.

"Yes. Wait, *no*. Daddy!" she cried and stomped her foot. "Sunday means church."

A pit formed in Liam's stomach. He should have nabbed that vodka when he'd had the chance. "Molly Sue, we don't go to church anymore," he explained, feeling like the absolute worst father in the whole world.

"Daddy, we have to go to church. God misses us."

Ouch. Sucker punch right to the gut. Somebody tag him out. There was no way he could argue with that.

"Okay, okay. I don't want to let God down," he said with a soft smile. "I'll go get ready. Please eat your pancakes while I do."

Molly Sue smiled back at him and jumped onto her bed, singing that *Frozen* song again and with more vigor than before. "For the first time in forever . . ." she belted out before stuffing a bite into her mouth and muffling her attempt to continue the song.

He listened to her clunky simultaneous performance of singing and eating as he tromped to his bedroom and began to look for something church appropriate. He never really left the house anymore. Most days he wore sweats or PJs, one of the best perks when it came to working from home, and—oh—he needed a shave and a haircut and . . .

"Are you almost ready, Daddy?" Molly Sue asked, appearing in the doorway.

"I don't know what to wear. It's been a long time since we've gone to church," he admitted.

She rolled her eyes again and marched toward his closet. "I know that, Daddy. It's why we have to go today . . . Wear this one," she said yanking on a garment tucked in the back of his closet.

He didn't have to look to know what it was—the suit he'd worn to Rebecca's funeral.

"Okay. Now get out of here so I can get dressed in private," he choked out.

Molly Sue skipped away happily, unaware of how upset she'd made her father. Liam tiptoed to his closest as if it held a monster he feared alerting to his presence. In a way, it did. That suit represented the worst day of his life. Why had he let it stay in his closet all these months? Why hadn't he burned the stupid thing the moment they'd come home from the funeral parlor?

He took the detested garment out of the closet, glanced over the smooth black fabric, and then threw it to the ground and kicked it under the bed. There, the dust bunnies should make a meal of that. For all the many beautiful memories he had, there were just as many he wished he could wipe clear from his mind, never to find them again. Maybe more of that second kind. They haunted him enough without him voluntarily letting the miserable suit grace his form.

No, he'd wear a polo shirt today. It was simply the best he could do, given the circumstances.

Hopefully his little girl would understand.

Molly Sue and Rebecca
Eighteen months ago

Five-year-old Molly Sue sat high up on her parents' bed, her back pushed against the large satin headboard. She liked how slippery it felt against her nightgown. Even more than that, she loved these special days when she got to stay home from school and spend the day relaxing with her mommy. They used to come only a couple of times per week, but lately she'd been home more days than she'd been away.

Every day had become a slumber party. She and Mommy both wore their jammies and stayed in bed watching princess movies and reading stories together. Today her mother wore the pajamas Molly Sue liked best from her large collection. They were purple—her very favorite color—and spotted with silly flying pigs all up and down the pant legs and even on the sleeves of the matching shirt. It always made Molly Sue laugh whenever she first caught a glimpse of her mommy in those PJs.

And laughing was good, because laughing meant you were happy.

Lately, both Mommy and Daddy had been crying . . . a lot.

They said her mother would be going away, going away forever. But in all her five and three-quarters years on this earth, Molly Sue had found that just because something feels like forever doesn't necessarily make it so. Like when she needed to potty while out for a drive, and she had to hold it so hard to wait for a toilet. It felt like forever, but eventually she got to empty her mean, old bladder. Or when she had waited and waited and waited some more for her favorite movie *Frozen* to come out on DVD. That really had been for forever! But now her movie was here, and she and Mommy were even watching it right now.

So when her parents said that Mommy would go away forever, she felt sad, but she also knew that forever wasn't for always, even though it sometimes felt that way.

"Molly," her mother whispered, lifting her arms up to draw Molly Sue into a cuddle. "Do you know how much I love you?"

Molly giggled. She loved this game. "One million."

"That's right. And do you know how long I will be with you?"

Molly Sue thought about this. A smile spread its way from cheek to cheek. She knew just the answer . . . at least she thought she did. "Forever?"

"Forever," her mother confirmed as she brushed the hair from Molly's face. Her eyes danced as they sometimes did when she got extra happy or extra sad.

"Even when I go to Heaven," her mother continued. "I'll still be here, too."

The little girl laughed again. "You can't be in two places at once, silly Mommy."

But Molly's mommy didn't laugh. Instead, a sad smile pinched her pretty features. "I'm going away, Molly Sue. My body is going away, but my spirit will live on in your heart and in Daddy's. Do you understand?"

She wasn't sure she did, but she nodded anyway. "When God is done visiting with you, can you come back?"

Mommy took a deep breath and drew her daughter near. She didn't say yes or no. Instead, she answered with, "We'll see each other again someday, I promise. But while I'm away, I'm going to need your help. Can you help me with something very important, Molly Sue?"

Molly sat up straight and pumped her head vigorously. She would do anything to help her mother, especially with how hard even the simplest things had been for her lately.

"Daddy is very sad," Mommy explained as she caressed the lacy frill on the sleeves of Molly Sue's nightie. "But you and I both know it's never too late for a fresh chance. That's why I need your help. Can you help be his angel when I go to Heaven? Can you help Daddy feel happy again?"

Well, yeah, of course! She wanted her daddy to be happy, almost more than anything in the whole wide world. "Yes, I can be Daddy's angel," she agreed.

"Good, because I have a plan . . ."

Jennifer had fewer pupils than normal that Sunday morning. Many were still away celebrating the holidays with out-of-town family members. Others had likely been claimed by the fresh strain of flu working its way up and down First Street. She liked days like this because the smaller group allowed for more intimate discussions.

For today's lesson, she'd decided to talk to the kids

about what happens after we get our miracles. It seemed fitting given that Christmas had just passed by and everyone had New Year's on the brain.

"So Jesus was born," she continued after a quick recap of the Christmas story. "The angels rejoiced, and the world was saved. What happened next?" she asked the children.

"The wise men came!" one of her older kids answered with a knowing smile.

"They did," she said, cocking her head to the side and offering a reassuring smile. "But what next?"

"Joy to the world!" A kindergartener popped to her feet and sang at the top of her lungs before collapsing in giggles.

"Yes." Jennifer smiled and nodded. "The world was happy, because it got its miracle. But what happens after the miracle has already come?"

Everyone grew quiet. Some of the children fidgeted in their seats. Others scratched their heads and tried to avoid eye contact.

"We don't know what you're talking about, Miss Elliot," one of her favorite students said in an exaggerated whisper that was actually louder than her normal indoor voice.

Jennifer laughed, and the children joined her. "It's a hard question to answer," she admitted. "Everyone always focuses on the miracle, on the happy ending.

But we all know that Jesus's birth wasn't the ending at all. In fact, it was just the beginning."

"So what did happen next?" Pastor Bernie's grandson asked, and Jennifer felt especially proud in that moment that she had managed to catch the little troublemaker's attention.

"Well, Jesus grew up into a little boy and then into a man," she said, placing her Bible on her lap and giving it a nice pat.

"And then he died-ed," one of the kids added.

"He did, but that's not the end either, is it?" Jennifer asked, leaning in close and wagging her finger. Her class always had more fun with the lessons when she made lots of big gestures and asked them to answer questions as she taught.

The pastor's grandson, Alex, stretched his hand high and waved it around as if waiting to be called on. "He came alive again on Easter!" he blurted out in excitement.

"He sure did, and He's alive even today, isn't He?"

The children nodded enthusiastically.

"Everyone focuses on the miracle of the birth this time of year, but you know what? Every day after that has been a miracle, too, because every day we are reminded of the promise God made to us, and every day He continues to keep that promise."

Josie raised her hand and shot a haughty look at

Alex when Jennifer called on her to share. "So are you saying every day is a new miracle?" she asked.

"That's exactly what I'm saying. Thank you for pointing that out, Josie. And I want you to all think about that as we move on past Christmas this year and then past the new year, too. Every single day is a new beginning. Every single day is a miracle, not just the ones we celebrate with presents and songs. Everybody got that?"

"Yes, Miss Elliott," the children sang more or less in unison.

"Good," she said, pressing down on her legs and rising from the small plastic chair. "I hear the grown-ups starting to move about out there. I think that means the big service is over. So . . . who would like to end our time together by saying a prayer?"

"Oooh, me! Me! Me!"

Many of the children wanted to lead the day's prayer, but none so enthusiastically as Josie, and Jennifer was happy to oblige her. Everyone bowed their heads, and Josie spoke her prayer quickly in a squeaky, excited voice.

"Dear God and Jesus. Thank you for loving us and taking away our sins, and thank you for my new Barbies, too. Amen."

"Amen," Jennifer said with a chuckle.

A few of the boys groaned.

"I'll see you all next week," Jennifer called after the departing children. "Make this a great one! And Happy New Year!" She watched them fly through the doors and into the waiting arms of their parents, thankful for another chance to mold their hearts this week.

"Molly Sue!" Josie cried in her squeaky shout. "We haven't seen you for forever."

Molly Sue? Could it really be? Jennifer craned her neck to see through the small throng of children congregating by the door, and sure enough, Molly Sue James stood with her father, Liam, just outside the classroom.

"Well, hello, stranger," she said, striding through the crowd of children and parents. She hadn't run into him since the grand reopening of Mabel's, though she'd often wondered if he'd ever take her up on her invite to rejoin the congregation at First Street Church.

"We were too late for Sunday school, but God is happy we came anyway, right?" Molly Sue asked with a pout.

"Of course He is, and I am, too, and so are all your friends here. We have really missed you." She stood a little straighter and tucked a strand of hair behind each ear. "Both of you," she added, then gave Molly Sue a hug and smiled at Liam—a hug felt too personal and a handshake felt too formal. And, oh, he looked handsome today, even though he clearly needed a shave and probably a haircut, too. She'd always liked men with a bit of scruff, and Liam's suited his strong jaw and high cheekbones.

"That's what I thought, too," Molly shouted. No wonder her and Josie were such good friends. "It's never too late for a fresh chance. That's what Mom told me, and I believe her." Molly Sue turned back to her friends, leaving Jennifer and Liam to talk.

"Did you forget what time church starts?" Jennifer teased to lighten the mood.

"I . . . No. I hadn't actually planned on coming at all, but Molly Sue insisted." His hazel eyes met hers, and she had to force herself to look away to avoid getting ensnared by them. No, no, she couldn't be attracted to her dead friend's husband. Talk about an inappropriate crush!

Maybe if she kept talking, she would stop focusing on how her body and heart responded to his strong presence. "You know, usually we get our EC Christians on Easter and Christmas. You missed it by one week."

He frowned and looked over at his daughter, who was immersed in an animated conversation with her friends.

"I'm sorry. I don't mean to give you a hard time.

It's just good to see you, is all. And Molly Sue, too, of course."

He frowned slightly and then forced a small smile. "Well, it seems we'll be back next week. Molly Sue is adamant on that. She said God misses us."

"Oh, seems you have no choice in the matter, then. Well, I'll be sure to give her a warm welcome to the class next week. Really, Liam, I do think it's good for both of you to be here. We need God most when . . ." She let her words fall away. She didn't need to remind him of all he had lost, not when the grief already clung to him like day-old cologne. "Well, we need God always, don't we?"

He smiled wanly. "Yes, I suppose we do. Anyway, we just wanted to stop in to say hello and that we'll see you next week." He turned from her and called to his daughter, "Molly Sue, time to say goodbye!"

The little girl trotted up breathlessly and yanked on her father's arm. "Daddy, are we going to the restaurant next? We used to always go to lunch after church, and I'm real hungry."

"I . . . sure."

"Oh, Miss Elliott? Will you come with us, too?" Molly asked, blinking up at Jennifer with an expression that didn't seem to have much of a question in it at all.

Jennifer looked from the smiling girl to her

scowling father. He quickly rearranged his face into a resigned grin, but not before Jennifer could catch the discomfort there. "Oh, I don't think that's such a—"

"Please, Miss Elliott? Please!" Molly Sue tugged at her arm. She was really quite strong for a seven-year-old and even caused Jennifer to stumble a little in her short heels.

She glanced quickly at Liam who gave a slight nod. "Well, of course, I'd be delighted, Miss Molly Sue," she answered with all the enthusiasm she could muster. For while she loved the little girl, she couldn't be certain how she felt about the father—and that uncertainty worried her greatly.

THREE

Liam couldn't be sure, but he *thought* he saw Molly Sue give him a quick wink after inviting Jennifer Elliott to join them for their Sunday lunch. And if she had, well . . . that would make absolutely no sense at all.

He and Molly both liked Jennifer. Of course they did. She had been one of Rebecca's closest friends—*Rebecca's*, not Liam's. Liam had always been more of the private type. He preferred the company of a book or a newspaper to that of other real, live people. And now it just felt strange to be claiming his dead wife's friends as his own or, rather, allowing Molly Sue to claim these friends for the both of them.

No, this wasn't right, especially considering the way his breathing had hitched just a little when he'd stood next to the Sunday school teacher in the door-way, that his heart had sped when she'd smiled at him, that . . .

No, no, not good, and definitely not what he wanted.

He was lonely. He missed his wife.

That was all.

So he'd have this lunch to humor his little girl, and then it would be over. And just in case she tried to pull this stunt again next week, he'd have an excuse on hand so that they could slip away from the sanctuary unaccompanied.

And, as for today, what could one little lunch hurt?

Jennifer had walked to church that morning, so she rode with Liam and Molly Sue to the restaurant, sitting quietly with her hands in her lap almost as if she didn't know where to put them. "Wait!" she cried, startling Liam and causing him to swerve slightly over the middle line of First Street. "You missed the turnoff for Mabel's."

"We're not going to Mabel's," he said with a grin he hoped appeared natural. "I thought it might be nice to visit Ernie's instead." *And it would definitely be nice to avoid running into the whole of Sweet Grove at Mabel's diner*, he mentally added. Ernie's would be quieter, less of a production.

The German restaurant wasn't often busy, but given the high cost of its meals and the fact it doubled as the local caterer, the business wasn't in danger of closing its doors anytime soon. Liam knew this for a fact because he had helped Ernie assess his overall business strategy and plan for the expansion into catering back when he'd first moved to town as a starry-eyed newlywed so many years ago.

It didn't take long at all to drive from the far south side of Sweet Grove all the way north to Ernie's out by the orchard. He parked right by the front door and briefly wondered whether he should run round to open the door for Jennifer, too.

Luckily, she unbuckled herself and quickly sprang to her feet outside, stretching her arms overhead. "I haven't been here in ages," she exclaimed, seemingly oblivious to how awkward this whole thing was for Liam. "I don't remember what's on the menu, but I'm excited to find out again. Are you ready, Molly Sue?"

He watched as she extended her hand to Molly Sue and walked with her into the restaurant, realizing a moment later that he'd missed another opportunity to open the door for her. *Oh well, it's for the best. I don't want her thinking this is a date . . . Wait. Why am I thinking like that? And now that I've brought her to the fanciest place in town will she . . . ? Not good, Liam, not good.*

He warred with himself as he trailed a few steps behind the girls. Apparently did a bad job hiding it, too, because Molly Sue let go of Jennifer's hand and rushed over to saddle him with a huge side hug.

"What's wrong, Daddy?"

"Just very, very hungry!" he said, returning the hug and then rubbing his stomach with big exaggerated pats to prove his point.

"Well, then you are in luck, because today's special is one of our most popular: beef roulade served on a bed of spaetzle with a special pickled red cabbage salad to start," the young waiter said, scooping up menus and directing them toward a table that overlooked the river.

"Tobias!" Jennifer squealed, wrapping her arms around him before taking her seat. "I didn't know you were in town!"

He pushed his dark hair back from his face and shrugged. "Just for the week. I'm helping Gramps out over the holidays, then it's back to the rigors of 3L life for me."

Her eyes widened, and she let out a low whistle. "Impressive, Mr. Lloyd. Very impressive. You've gotta be almost finished, right? You've been in school forever."

Liam felt his stomach growl, not with hunger but rather envy. Jennifer had come out with him but now directed all her attention toward Ernie's young and handsome grandson. *Wait, it's okay. We're not on a date. Just friends, and just because my daughter forced us into this.* He didn't like how often he needed to remind himself where he stood with Jennifer. It made him feel like the worst sort of husband and the worst sort of person, too.

Tobias and Jennifer continued their upbeat exchange while Liam forced himself to remain quiet and to keep a friendly, nonjealous smile plastered on his face.

"I'm graduating this spring, actually," Tobias boasted—at least, it seemed like boasting to Liam. After all, he didn't go around shouting out his credentials for all to hear. "I bet you my mom wouldn't feel like my life is such a waste of space now. Not if she saw what I've been able to make of myself despite everything!"

Jennifer placed a reassuring hand on the waiter's arm, and the two of them caught each other's eyes. "She'd be very proud, I know it. I mean, I'm proud of you. We all are."

Liam bristled. He knew this wasn't a date, but did this other fellow know that? If not, he was definitely taking too many liberties here. He cleared his throat and offered a polite but firm smile again.

Tobias nodded pertly and laid the menus on the

table at last. "Oh, anyway, enough about me. I'll bring you a glass of the house Riesling while you have a look at the menu." He stalked away without a smile.

Jennifer frowned as she unfolded the cloth napkin and smoothed it across her lap.

Oh, maybe he had been the one to take too many liberties. It's not a date, and they're obviously old friends. Why did he have to be rude like that? Ugh, this is why he preferred to stay locked in his office as often as he possibly could. He needed a way to get back in Jennifer's good graces to show he meant no harm.

"That's Ernie's grandson, right?" he asked, gesturing across the restaurant in the direction Tobias had gone. "I never would have guessed. He doesn't look a thing like the old man."

"Well, his dad is from Mexico, and . . . Well, I don't like to gossip. Not when there are so many cheerier things to talk about. Like you finally coming back to us, Miss Molly Sue!" She turned to face Molly, who sat beside her and talked animatedly with her hands. "Thank you for inviting me to lunch. This is all very exciting! Did you get any good Christmas presents?"

Yes, talk to Molly Sue. At least she won't act like a jealous fool.

Molly Sue shrugged and began to swing her feet

back and forth under the table. "The usual—clothes, toys, art supplies."

Jennifer shot Liam a quizzical expression. "What about New Year's? Have you made any big plans?"

"No, we don't get out much," his daughter said with a frown that cut straight to his heart. "Hey, maybe you would like to come over to our house to celebrate?" she suggested, and there it was again. This time, Liam *definitely* saw a wink.

"I would love to, Molly Sue, but I already have plans with my friends. Say, do you have any special resolutions this year?"

Molly nodded vigorously. "I do, but I can't tell yet."

"Oh, a secret resolution? That's exciting."

"Yup." *Wink.*

"How about you, Liam?" Jennifer asked, lifting her gaze to catch him staring at her.

He cleared his throat in an effort to stall for time. He was doing that a lot today. Where was the smooth confident business man, and why had he been replaced by this bumbling imposter on today of all days?

"Um, Liam?" Jennifer asked with a reassuring bob of her head. "Resolutions?"

Oh, he'd zoned out again. Good thing he was only on a . . . out with an old friend and not meeting with a new client today. If so, he'd have already lost out on that deal many times over.

Jennifer chuckled softly and took a long, slow gulp of water.

His little girl shot daggers at him from across the table.

Oh, that's right! She asked about my New Year's resolution.

Well, it wouldn't do any good to explain that he no longer had any hopes or dreams for himself, thus making something as silly as resolutions absolutely pointless—and he definitely didn't want to say that in front of his impressionable daughter, either. So instead he shrugged and said, "Isn't it obvious? To come to church every week."

Molly Sue grinned so big it highlighted the missing teeth on both sides of her mouth. "And what about you, Miss Elliott?"

"Oh, me?" Jennifer put down her water goblet and picked up her wine glass. Liam couldn't help but feel she was stalling as well. "I actually don't have any New *Year's* resolutions," she answered thoughtfully.

Liam saw his own confusion was mirrored in Molly's twisted-up face.

Jennifer laughed. "I don't make resolutions for the new year. I make them for the new day, every day. Every day can be the very best day of your life if you let it, so that's my promise to myself: that each day I'll let life come at me and be open to what it has to offer."

Hmmm. Well, that explained a lot. Rebecca had once lived like that, too, until her life was cut short. Fat load of good the free-spirit, happy-go-lucky stuff did. Instead of keeping her safe, it meant his wife had a more difficult time accepting the end.

And Jennifer was exactly the same.

No wonder he liked her so much even though he had every reason not to. No wonder she made him feel like a hopeless, lovesick teenager. No wonder he actually kind of did wish this were a date after all.

Jennifer watched as Molly Sue scribbled furiously on her placemat, a vibrant swirl of red, blue, green, and orange. Ernie's was a fancy restaurant with cloth napkins and lacy tablecloths, but they still always had crayons on hand for any children who happened by.

"What are you drawing?" she asked to break the silence that had set in once again.

The little girl looked up for a split second, then threw herself back into her work. "You'll see." She smiled as she drew, and Jennifer couldn't help but wonder if she might be up to something naughty.

Liam cleared his throat beside her. "Did you like your meal?" he asked, gesturing toward her half-eaten plate of schnitzel. "I'm paying, of course."

"What? No. I mean, *yes*. I liked the meal, and, *no*, you aren't paying. Don't be silly."

"But I invited you," he argued.

"Actually, Molly Sue did, and I don't mind paying my own way, really." She had to be firm here. Yeah, this meal was expensive, but she was the one who had agreed to come. She was the one whose belly had been filled.

Tobias rushed over with a to-go box and the check. "Split it, please," she said, handing him her battered Visa card. It had seen a rough few months, that was for sure.

"Certainly," Tobias answered before disappearing with both her and Liam's cards.

"You didn't need to do that." He frowned and cracked his knuckles. A nervous gesture, perhaps? Jennifer hadn't made anyone nervous in all her life. What had changed now?

"Yes, I did," she said with a placating smile. "We're friends out to lunch, not a date." Oops, why did she say that? They weren't on a date, that much was true, but did she have to put the word out there?

Especially in front of Molly Sue, who just continued to grin as she worked on her picture?

She still remembered Rebecca calling her, breathless with excitement upon returning from her first date with Liam. *He held the door open and everything. Such a gentleman!* her friend had gushed.

She also recalled their wedding, the one she had been a part of in her baby-pink satin dress with white elbow-length gloves and bits of baby's breath in her hair. Liam's eyes had sparkled then as he said his I do's. Now they were dull and dark, a never-ending abyss of sorrow. How much the years can change a person, she thought, realizing at the same time she had remained exactly the same.

If only he would smile again, smile and mean it. He was so handsome back then, so happy. And he deserves that now, to be happy. If only I could help . . .

Help with what? She scolded herself. *Kiss away his tears? Ridiculous. Ridiculous and moreover very, very wrong.*

She could be his friend, as she had been for his late wife. But not if she continued to find herself swooning after him like this. Even this simple friendly lunch put her in dangerous territory. She wanted to help, but she also didn't know how to deal with grief as deep as Liam's. She didn't know whether it was okay to talk about Rebecca or if doing so would only make him hurt more. She didn't know whether offering him a reassuring hug was a nice, friendly gesture, or if the fact that her heart sped up when she thought about touching him made it a selfish, sinful thing instead.

So many questions, and not even close to enough answers.

"Are you all right, Jennifer?" Liam asked, leaning forward to search her eyes. "You seem lost."

She forced a laugh, hoping it sounded natural. "I'm right here. Hey, Molly, can we see your picture now?"

Molly leaned across the table and pushed her drawing toward Jennifer. "I made this for you." She beamed as both Jennifer and Liam took in the image of an angel flying through a sunset sky.

"It's beautiful," she said on a slow exhale. "Is this your mom?"

"Sure is!" Molly Sue announced proudly.

"Do you think of your mom like that? As an angel?" Clearly the child wanted to talk about her mother, whether or not her father shared that same desire.

Liam shifted in his chair beside her. "I'm going to the restroom."

Molly Sue didn't miss a beat. "I know Mommy is an angel because she told me. I'm an angel, too."

"You are? But I don't see any wings." Jennifer searched from side to side, eliciting a giggle from the little girl. "And, hey, where's your halo?"

"I'm a different kind of angel. I'm Daddy's angel."

Oh my gosh, this is the cutest thing ever. Liam had to be a good dad to have such a great kid, a fact which made her like him even better.

"You definitely are. Your daddy loves you so very much," she agreed before inhaling the last few drops of her wine.

"Yeah . . ." Molly's shoulders fell and she mumbled toward the ground. "But he never wants to talk about Mommy anymore. That makes it very hard."

"Hard on you? Do you want to talk about your mom? You know you can talk to me about her any time, right? Any time at all, I mean it."

The little girl sighed and looked back up at Jennifer with huge, shaky eyes. "Thank you, Miss Elliott. I do miss my mommy a lot, but I meant something else."

"What did—"

"It makes it hard for me to do the job Mommy asked me to do."

A job? Well, this was unexpected. When Molly Sue didn't continue, Jennifer decided to gently nudge her. "What did she—"

"Ready to go?" Liam cut in, returning to the table and gesturing for Molly Sue to stand.

Molly Sue nodded and raced around the table with her drawing in hand. "This is for you, Miss Elliott," she said, pressing the picture into Jennifer's hands. "Mommy wants you to have it."

All traces of the lingering sadness had once again disappeared, and Molly Sue had transformed back into a happy, carefree child. At least for now.

"That's very nice of you both," Jennifer exclaimed. "Thank you, Molly Sue," she said as she gave the little girl a hug. "Thank you, too, Rebecca," she said, lifting her face toward Heaven. Was her friend there listening now? And what would she think of the romantic thoughts Jennifer had begun to harbor for her husband? Would her friend even recognize her anymore?

She'd prefer not to find out.

It was a good thing only kids attended her Sunday school class, because she wanted more than anything to be there for Molly Sue. But perhaps every bit as much she wanted to stay far, far away from Liam . . . except she didn't actually want that at all.

FOUR

L iam couldn't get Jennifer out of his car fast enough. It wasn't that he hadn't enjoyed their meal together. No, even with all the awkward pauses and the whole ordeal over who should pay, he'd liked spending time with her.

And that was the problem.

Liam owed Rebecca his loyalty. After all, he'd taken a vow. *Until death do us part.* Rebecca had crossed that bridge already, but *he* wasn't dead yet—and in his heart, he remained very much married.

Noticing the way Jennifer's skirts swished against her calves as she ran toward her apartment door, watching as she smiled and greeted a neighbor, wondering why he hadn't realized before that her eyes were a special shade of cobalt he found rather soothing . . .

All of it. Wrong.

He would never have cheated on Rebecca in life, and the fact that his mind's eye had envisioned taking Jennifer in his arms, dipping her back, and kissing her . . . So, so wrong. Especially because Liam knew with every fiber in his being that Rebecca was up in Heaven watching him and Molly Sue live their lives here on Earth.

She would see everything. Perhaps she'd already witnessed his unclean thoughts for the Sunday school teacher.

No, no, no.

He was just lonely. That had to be it. He missed his wife. Her friend had become a natural substitute for his daydreams, but she was also the worst possible choice when it came to actually pursuing a relationship again.

Not that he would do that.

No, he didn't need anybody. He had his little girl, his work, and the memory of what love had felt like. It would have to be enough. Otherwise, he wouldn't be able to so much look at himself in the mirror.

Molly reached forward in the back seat and drummed her hands on the armrest beside him. "Can we put on my music?" A slight pause. "*Please!*" she said through a huge grin, knowing he couldn't resist when she took extra strides to be polite.

He allowed himself one last glance at Jennifer, who still stood chatting with the neighbor. The animated gestures she made when talking, the huge smile, everything about the way Jennifer carried herself proved she had what he did not: *happiness*.

Toddling after these new feelings for her would not only dishonor Rebecca's memory, but also end up hurting Jennifer, too. How could she be happy with an anchor dragging her down into his sorrow? Yes, he was just lonely, he decided, as he hooked his iPhone up to the charging cable and thumbed over to Molly's playlist. Taylor Swift's "Shake It Off" blasted through the speaker, and Molly joined in with a rousing rendition of her own.

"Shake It Off." "Let It Go." Even his child's music knew the right call here. If his loneliness didn't go away soon, maybe he could join a book club or take on a local client or two. He needed human interaction, not romance.

When the song ended, Molly Sue leaned forward again so that she was speaking almost directly into his ear. "Daddy, don't you think—"

"Back in your seat, Little Miss!" he warned as he turned onto Main Street.

She groaned, and he watched as she theatrically

thumped herself back against the seat. "Like I was saying . . ." She caught his eye in the rearview mirror and smiled. "Don't you think Miss Elliott is really pretty? I loved her dress, and she has the nicest hair."

"Um, sure."

"It's okay, Daddy. You can say she's not pretty if that's what you think."

"I didn't say—"

"So you *do* think she's pretty!" Molly sunk back farther in her seat with a triumphant smile on her face. Was he so obvious that his seven-year-old, who didn't know the first thing about crushes, could detect his? He had to be careful how he answered. Otherwise, he'd never hear the end of it.

"Miss Elliott is . . ." he mumbled, "attractive. *Sure*."

"I knew it! And by the way, Daddy, I think so, too. Miss Elliott is super pretty and funny and nice and smart, and she was one of Mommy's best friends, too, wasn't she?" She hurried through her words, not stopping to take a breath until the very end.

"Yes," he confirmed. "Your mother and Miss Elliott were close growing up."

"Mommy has good taste in friends. I like Miss Elliott." She winked at him in the rearview mirror. So that's what all this was about! His daughter had decided to play matchmaker. She must have gotten the idea from one of those shows she liked to watch on the Disney channel. That had to be it. If he didn't encourage her, she'd drop it and move on to her next infatuation.

"Okay, great," he said, trying to match her excitement as he artfully redirected their conversation. "I'm glad you had fun today. You'll see her next week at church, too, but we won't be able to do lunch again. I have a lot of work to get to and can't spend the whole day in town. Okay?"

"Okay, Daddy." Molly continued to smile as she turned her gaze toward the long line of trees outside the window. Other than bursting into the occasional song when one of her favorite tracks played, she stayed quiet for most of the remaining drive home.

It gave Liam time to his thoughts, which he had to keep forcing away from Jennifer. Of course he was thinking about her. She was one of the few real-life people he saw these days. So many of his interactions happened online or over the phone, and she was one of the only age-appropriate women he'd seen for months. The tutor was too young, and the cleaning lady was too old, and . . .

He stopped himself. Age appropriate? What did he mean by that?

When finally they reached home, he fled to his office, leaving Molly Sue to her own devices. Hopefully she'd find a way to distract herself and get Jennifer off her brain, too. He dove into his work but found himself making careless mistakes as he attempted to navigate a new client's P&L statement.

Jennifer danced through his mind, and suddenly he was recalling memories he hadn't realized he'd saved. Meeting her the first time when he came to Sweet Grove with Rebecca to see the town where she'd grown up, watching Jennifer dance with his granddad at the wedding reception and cry soft tears at the funeral—he'd filed it all away, and it tormented him now.

He needed to scrub the memories from his brain before they became more permanent fixtures, and so he pulled out his iPad and loaded up his emergency library, then lost the rest of the night flicking through videos and photos and even old voicemail messages he'd saved from Rebecca.

These were the memories that mattered. These were the ones he'd fight like hell to protect.

Jennifer scrolled through her Facebook feed while chewing on her hair, something she only did when stressed to the max. Catching herself in the act, she spat out the soaked tendril and frowned. Liam had gotten into her head—not good. Still no updates from Jessica or her parents—also not good.

She needed a distraction, but calling up her sister and likely being lectured about how long it had been since her last visit to Maryland would not be pleasant. Nor would talking with her mother and being similarly lectured on her complete absence of a love life or a lucrative job when her perfect sister had already accomplished everything under the sun.

What would make me happy right now?

Jennifer glanced back at the computer and spotted a before-and-after pic Kristina Rose had just posted showing off her latest weight loss goal. *Perfect.*

Her "dumb phone"—so called because it was plain and ordinary, with no extra bells or whistles like the phones of her friends—sat where she'd thrown it on the kitchen counter. She bounded over to it and placed a call to Kristina Rose.

"Hey, you sexy beast!" Jennifer shouted into the receiver. "Size twelve now? That's so awesome! Let's go shopping to celebrate. Want to?"

"You had me at *sexy beast*," Kristina Rose answered with a giggle. "I know Elise is busy prepping for her youth service tonight, but I bet Summer and Maisie will come, too. Should we hit the outlet mall in Herald Springs?"

"Sounds like a plan. Can you swing by and pick me up? My car's making this weird rattling noise, and I'd prefer not to take it on the highway if I can avoid that."

"Sure thing. See you soon!"

When they hung up, Jennifer changed into jeans and a cute T-shirt she'd picked up during back-to-school season.

Close to an hour later, they were all at the mall trying on clothes in the big-box department store whose perfumed air Jennifer couldn't afford to breathe. She stayed quiet, though, since this was *her* problem and not something she wanted to bother her friends about.

"I can't believe how amazing you look!" she squealed when Kristina Rose emerged from the fitting room wearing a swanky A-line dress.

Kristina Rose twirled in front of the others, and Jennifer let out a wolf whistle. Maisie clapped, and Summer whooped from inside her own dressing room.

"I can't believe this is really me," Kristina admitted.

"Well, you better believe it, sugar," Jennifer teased.

"Jennifer, no sugar!" Maisie play-slapped her. "She's diabetic, remember?"

Everyone erupted in giggles.

"Ladies, tell me what you think, and be honest!" Summer called from behind the changing curtain.

Kristina fought back her blushed cheek and turned to wait for Summer's appearance. "Well, get your butt out here and we'll tell you!"

Their friend appeared, walking slowly on bare feet. The dress she wore fell all the way to the floor and was either deep red or shiny black, depending on how it caught the light. A row of gems adorned the neckline, highlighting the ample cleavage Jennifer hadn't realized Summer possessed. The whole effect was stunning.

"Oh, Summer, wow. That dress was made for you," Kristina Rose whispered as if in reverence.

"What's it for?" Maisie asked.

Summer studied herself in the angled set of mirrors. "I know it's a bit early, but I've just been thinking about Ben's and my first Valentine's Day. Do you think I should get it?"

"You'd better!" Kristina Rose and Maisie both shouted.

Summer smiled and turned toward Jennifer. "What do you think?"

"It's true. You look amazing, but that dress is very fancy. Where is Ben taking you for Valentine's Day?" Jennifer longed to wear such a beautiful gown herself, and she was half-tempted to try it on. But why do that to herself when she'd never be able to afford such a luxury, let alone have any place to wear it? That didn't stop her from daydreaming about wearing a similar blue dress of her own while proudly gripping Liam's strong arm as he twirled her in a dance. His cummerbund, of course, matched the blue in her dress perfectly. What a lovely, albeit completely imaginary, couple they made.

Summer laughed, bringing Jennifer's brief flight of fancy crashing to the ground. "I don't actually know yet. It's ridiculous, but I just felt like this dress was calling to me. Like I needed to have it, and it was somehow perfect for the plans we haven't even made yet."

"I know what you mean," Kristina Rose said. "I've had a goal dress hanging in my closet for years, way before I even thought the surgery might be a possibility. It's short and gold and crazy sexy. One day I'm going to make a great memory wearing that dress."

"Are you going to get anything, Jenn?" Maisie studied Jennifer while chewing on a stray hangnail.

Jennifer put on a smile though the memory of the hole tugging at her dress's neck earlier that morning made her want to cry. "Oh, I don't really need any clothes." She hated to be the odd one out, especially since this whole trip had been her idea, so she added,

"But you know what? I did see a pair of earrings I loved. Maybe I'll get those."

"Good! Now can we hit the food courts? I am famished," Maisie said theatrically, as she said most things.

"Hang on! I have to change back." Summer waddled quickly toward the dressing room with Kristina Rose in close pursuit.

"Me, too!"

"Meet you upfront," Maisie called, grabbing Jennifer's hand and tugging her toward the registers. They found a pair of earrings Jennifer liked and then waited for the others.

Once Summer's and Kristina Rose's dresses had been carefully wrapped into a plastic garment bag emblazoned with the store's logo, Jennifer slid her earrings across the counter toward the cashier.

"Is that it?" she asked, her eyes fixed on Jennifer's empty hands.

"Yes. Oh, wait. I have a coupon for ten percent off." Jennifer shifted her weight from one foot to the other while she waited for the cashier to finish ringing her up. *Please go through, please go through*, she prayed.

The cashier frowned and shook her head. "I'm sorry, but this card's getting declined. Do you have another?"

"Can you try again?" Jennifer's heart dropped to her feet.

"I already did."

"Hey, Jennifer, it's okay. Let me," Maisie offered, handing the cashier a twenty.

Jennifer felt the heat rise to her cheeks. If only it could lift her up and out of here like a hot air balloon. "Thank you," she mumbled, taking the small bag for the even smaller purchase she couldn't afford to make on her own.

"You didn't have to do that," she whispered to Maisie as they headed back into the ebb and flow of mall traffic.

"It's fine. It was only a few dollars, and besides, your credit card company probably just made a mistake anyway. Don't worry about it."

But Jennifer was worried about it—very worried. She knew the lunch at Ernie's that afternoon had been too much, even with her saving half to bring home. She'd blown her food budget for the next two weeks and maxed out her card all in one stupid, pig-headed transaction. She should have just let Liam pay.

But now she'd need to be creative with her spending for the month in order to cover her bills and afford to pay her friend back, too. The money would come—it always did—but that didn't make it any less stressful while waiting on her next paycheck to come in.

So she had rent and student loans, and she needed to eat and pay insurance, but it was just money. One thing she knew for sure was that no one ever seemed to have enough. Making more also seemed to mean *spending* more, too, a vicious cycle if ever there was one.

She'd find a way. Finances were the least—if not the most persistent—of her troubles. There was no need to change her perfect life for something as imperfect as money.

Wealth didn't make people happy. Liam James was proof enough of that . . . And now he was on her mind again. *Oh God, will I ever find a distraction that works?*

FIVE

The beginnings of a headache crowded Liam's temples. Between the guilt, the worry, and the unwanted crush, he hadn't slept well for the past several nights. He'd also been avoiding Molly Sue as much as possible, and that only added to the massive weight on his heart.

He just didn't know how to connect with her these days, especially with all this new Jennifer nonsense. Even if he was a less than adequate father, he could still be an exceptional provider. Work made sense—it always had. Putting in long hours meant more money, and more money meant a comfortable upbringing for Molly Sue and, eventually, a sizeable inheritance as well.

The pain burrowed deeper into his skull. Seemed

the Excedrin he'd taken earlier was doing nothing to stave off this migraine. He needed to push through, considering he was no good to anyone if he spent the day sleeping off the throbbing ache in his brain.

A burst of new messages appeared in his e-mail inbox, giving him plenty to distract himself. Someone needed to move up the deadline on his quarterly evaluation. Someone else had a new product coming to market and needed a full launch proposal, and another client needed an ROI statement for his consulting services to date by the close of business. It would be a busy day, to say the least.

He sighed and tucked in with work for the latter client. Despite Liam's glowing recommendations and stellar performance, this particular CEO always doubted the value he brought to her company. That's why he'd be delivering a letter of resignation along with the report that day. With a waiting list a digital mile long, he didn't need to take guff from anyone— least of all a business owner who was every bit as neurotic as she was inept.

Somewhere in the midst of crunching all the necessary numbers, a knock sounded on his office door.

"Come in," he called, rubbing at his temples as he spun in his chair to face the visitor.

Molly Sue's private tutor hovered uncomfortably

in the doorway, a single steno notebook clutched to her chest. "Mr. James, I'm sorry to interrupt, but I need to talk with you."

"Of course, Megan. Is everything all right?"

The girl's lack of eye contact and notably quick-ened breath suggested bad news was on its way. "Um, yes and no. Friday will be my last day teaching Molly Sue."

Too many words crowded his brain all at once. Only one managed to escape: "Why?"

Megan mumbled as she glanced back toward the door, playing the deer in headlights even though she'd been the one to summon the car. "I'm really sorry. Molly Sue is a great kid, but a last-minute spot opened up in the study abroad program this semester and I'm going to Paris."

"I'll pay you more," he insisted, hoping his desperation wasn't too off-putting. "How much will it take? Please, Molly Sue needs you."

"You've always been fair to me, Mr. James, and I appreciate the opportunity, but it's not about the money. I get to live in Paris while working toward my degree. How could I pass up an opportunity like that when I know it's not a chance I'll ever have again?"

"Could you at least give me two weeks' notice so I can find someone else to take over?" Liam had always been a fair employer. He paid well and offered praise frequently. He planned to give his problem client a full month's notice, yet somehow his own employee could only offer two days?

"The program starts next week, so no. I can't." Megan eyed him cautiously as she pushed her open notebook toward him. "Look, I've talked with a few friends who major in education, too, and may be able to take my place. But . . ."

"But what?"

"I really think you should consider enrolling Molly Sue in school again. She's just alone too much. She needs other kids in her life, needs the socialization opportunity. I don't mean to criticize, but she can't live her whole life trapped inside these four walls. She deserves better than that. Don't you think?"

Liam might have been angry if he weren't so sad. Of course Megan was right, but sending his little girl back to school felt like erasing another memory of Rebecca, writing over more of her story.

Megan had been a part of that story, too. She'd helped share the load with Rebecca in her final months. She knew their situation, their pain, and now she was leaving them, too. Liam's head throbbed as if to remind him that he had more than one kind of pain to manage that day.

Bringing in someone new would mean reopening

wounds that still bled. Eventually there'd be no life force left within him at all.

At least then he'd be with Rebecca again.

* * *

Molly Sue and Rebecca
Sixteen months ago

Molly Sue looked out at her big yard through the big window in her big house. The heat danced near the driveway as it so often did on hot summer days. When that happened, she liked to pretend she was underwater, a mermaid living in a coral castle rather than a little girl living in the woods outside of town.

Soon school would start again, and she would be one of the big kids. First grade! That meant she'd be at school all day instead of just a half day. She felt equal parts excited and sad. She loved learning and seeing her friends, but she would also miss spending the full days with her mommy. Mommy could leave for Heaven anytime, and then Molly Sue wouldn't see her again for a very long time. She understood that better now, and whenever she thought about it, she'd sneak away to her room to cry into her Elsa bedcovers.

But she wasn't going to think about it now. No

siree bob! She had to be brave and strong and good like her mommy had asked her to be. It was all part of her angel training.

"Molly Sue," her father said, laying a hand on her shoulder from behind.

She jumped back, startled. She hadn't heard him leave his office or come down the stairs or tiptoe up to her at the window.

"Sorry, I didn't mean to scare you." He smiled and held out his arms for a hug, which Molly Sue gladly returned. She liked to squeeze as hard as her muscles could to see if she could knock all the air out of her big, strong daddy. He always pretended it worked, but Molly knew he was faking.

"Oof!" Daddy said, letting out a giant puff of air like the big, bad wolf, except happy and friendly, not scary or in the mood to eat little piglets.

She giggled even though she still felt sad about Mommy inside her heart. If they were all mermaids like Ariel, would the cancer have been able to find Mama deep under the sea? Or would they all be able to live happily ever after like in the movies?

Sometimes—even lots of times—mommies died in the movies, and everyone still ended up happy when the story ended. Did that mean Molly Sue would be happy, too, like Cinderella or Elsa or Bambi? Why did mommies have to die so much, and was it her fault since she had secretly wished to be a princess when she blew out her birthday candles?

"Hey, what's on your mind?" her daddy asked, giving her a playful jab on the shoulder.

She smiled up at him and stuck her tongue through the place where her tooth was missing at the front of her mouth. "Mermaids," she answered honestly.

He laughed. "That was not an answer I expected. Love you, kiddo. Now, hey, your mom wants to see you in our room. Better head on up."

She nodded, returned the I love yous, gave him another tight, wind-knocker-outer hug, and skipped up the stairs.

"There she is," Mommy said with her quiet inside voice. She patted the bed next to her. "Hop on up. I want to talk to you."

Molly scrambled onto the bed and waited for her mommy to reveal whatever secret she had. At least she hoped it was a secret and not that she was in trouble.

Her mother smiled and pushed the hair behind Molly Sue's ears—big ears, but not big enough to fly like Dumbo. "You know that summer is almost over, right?"

Molly Sue pumped her head up and down. "Yes, and school starts, too!"

Mommy frowned. "That's what I wanted to talk

to you about. Daddy and I have decided not to send you to school this year."

"What? Then how will I get smart?"

"You already are smart, silly girl. If it's okay with you, we want to keep you home. And I'll be your teacher."

"So everyone will come to school at our house?"

"No, sweetie. Just you and me. Is that okay?"

"Is this because you have to go to Heaven?"

Her mother nodded. "Yes, and also because I'm selfish and want to keep you all to myself."

"I'm selfish, too, Mommy," Molly Sue said, snuggling into her mother's embrace.

"See, I knew we were just alike, you and me," Mommy said with a wink. "School doesn't start until next week, so how about we make some popcorn and watch a movie instead? What movie should we pick?"

Molly Sue thought long and hard about all her favorite movies. It took her a while to find one where the mommy doesn't die and everyone still gets to live happily ever after. "How about *Tangled*?"

"That's the perfect choice," her mother answered.

Jennifer worked her long blonde hair into a braid. She always woke up at seven on the nose, which gave her precious little time to get ready on work days, but she preferred being well rested to falsifying a fresh face. After all, what did the toddlers in her class care whether she applied eyeshadow and mascara?

She wrote out a quick check for half her month's rent along with an apology to her landlord, taking extra care to dot the *i*'s in her first and last name with hearts. Being around kids all day long did keep the whimsy alive, but she also held on to the hearts to pay homage to her late friend.

Back when they had been in school, and Rebecca James still went by Becky White, they had both written their names this way. In fact, Jennifer had adopted the signature specifically because she'd seen Rebecca sign hers in the same way.

Jennifer had always liked the older girl, who'd started as her sister's friend but quickly became hers as well. They'd become closer still, once Rebecca had returned from college with Liam in tow—an event that synced up almost exactly with her sister's big move out to Baltimore. And so, Rebecca had filled the newly vacated spot in Jennifer's life, becoming so much more than just a friend, but also something of a sister.

Funny how much things changed. First Jessica had gone, then Rebecca, and now here was Jennifer, carrying on the same as ever. She still had dear friends in Maisie, Elise, Summer, and Kristina Rose, but it just wasn't the same as it had been with Rebecca.

"I'm sorry," she whispered to the wind as she tucked the letter and check into her mailbox and put the flag up. "I'll have the rest soon," she promised before skipping off toward the daycare. If she lingered here any longer, she'd miss the first kids arriving for the day. Besides, it was her duty to open up shop on Fridays.

Better late with money than time. At least money could eventually be repaid.

Her landlord, Jonas Bryant, would surely understand, and if for some reason he didn't? Well, Jennifer could sic his sister Maisie on him to make her case.

Yup, everything would be A-OK.

"Good morning, Jennifer," the daycare owner, Patsy Carroll, said, welcoming her the moment she unlocked the door.

"Oh, Patsy. I didn't expect to see you so early today. To what do I owe the pleasure?" Jennifer smiled, but Patsy did not. In fact, the creases on her forehead were the deepest Jennifer had ever seen them in more than three years of working together at the Kitty Kids Daycare. Normally the creases only came out around quarterly tax time, so Jennifer knew whatever news her boss had to share that morning couldn't be good.

"Come in. Sit." Patsy motioned toward the tiny office she kept near the front of the building.

Jennifer followed her silently and took a seat. The kittens that adorned the pink wallpaper seemed to know something she hadn't figured out yet. How could kitties playing with yarn feel so menacing? The old Felix clock flicked its tail back and forth as it counted down the seconds to whatever big reveal Patsy had planned.

Jennifer hated the suspense. "You have me nervous, Patsy," she said as her boss set a mug of coffee before each of them. "What's going on?"

The older woman frowned as she folded her hands before her. "Jennifer, you've always been a tremendous asset to the daycare. The kids love you. You bring more creativity and enthusiasm than I could have ever hoped to ask for. Heck, I've even written you into my will. When I go, I can't imagine anyone other than you taking this place over . . ."

"Oh, that's so generous. Thank you so much for having faith in me." *Is Patsy sick? Is that what she wants to tell me?* Suddenly, Jennifer felt very, very sad.

Patsy sighed. "Jennifer, please. This is hard enough as is."

"I'm sorry. I didn't . . . Please go ahead." Jennifer tried to relax in her seat, but the tension kept her rooted in place.

"I can't afford to keep you full-time anymore. The kids we have are moving on to elementary school, and we don't have enough new children coming in. Paying benefits is expensive, and as much as I love you, I just can't justify the costs. As it is, I can barely afford to pay the bills as they come in, but you know how it is. We do it because we love the kids. I know Kitty Kids has become like a home to you, and I hate that I have no other choice. I've tried everything, but . . ." The creases came back, and Jennifer hated how upset her mentor had become on her account.

"If you'd like to stay part-time, you are certainly welcome. I do suggest you find a new job to help make ends meet. If that means you can't stay at Kitty Kids, I completely understand."

Jennifer's spine slowly softened as she slumped back in her chair. Patsy was okay, or at least she wasn't dying, so that was good. But what would Jennifer do with her days now? How would she make enough to pay the past-due rent or to finance her life going forward?

Patsy lifted her mug with shaking fingers. "Jennifer? Please say something. I feel terrible."

Jennifer lifted hers, too, and put on a smile. "Don't. I appreciate everything you've done for me over the years. I understand how hard it is when there's not enough money, but I'll find something new. It'll be okay," she promised.

"How about a toast?" she suggested when Patsy sat in silence. She raised her coffee mug higher. "To new beginnings and new adventures."

Patsy reluctantly clinked her mug against Jennifer's. "How are you always so upbeat? This has been killing me for weeks, and you don't seem upset."

Jennifer shrugged. "Life is better when you expect the best from it. Besides, I know God has got my back. Everything is going to be just fine. Don't you worry about me."

SIX

Liam hated new beginnings, mostly because they often meant trouble. Running into a car accident on his way to Sweet Grove Elementary School didn't exactly ease his tension, either. Seemed someone had clipped Beckett Hill on a wide left turn —and he did not look happy about it. As a teen, Liam had often worked alongside his father to restore a classic Camaro that hadn't seen the road in years. For all he knew, his dad was still plugging away, telling himself that any day now would be *the day* he finally took the old girl for a spin.

Liam chuckled to himself as he pulled into the sprawling school parking lot. He missed his parents whenever he spared a moment to think of them, but he couldn't exactly get away from work, nor did he want to be subjected to their obvious pity for what his life had become. He knew it was bad, but he couldn't do much of anything to fix it either.

Well, getting Molly Sue enrolled for second grade would be a start, and he had to make that start today, seeing as his daughter and her soon-to-be-former tutor were wrapping up their final lessons back at home. He trudged into the single-story brick building, the very same school his wife had attended back in her elementary days. The thought sent a shiver clear through him.

"Why, hey there, Mr. James." Someone he didn't recognize greeted him as he passed through the halls. *Man, I really am out of touch.*

He grumbled his hello and carried on until he found the principal's office.

"Hi. I called in yesterday. I need to register my daughter to join your second-grade class starting Monday," he told the elderly male receptionist who sat at the front desk.

"Yes, Molly Sue James." He broke out into a wide grin. *News certainly traveled fast around this town.* "We're happy to have her. Principal Perkins is just finishing up with another meeting. Can you have a seat until she's ready, please?"

He took a seat as instructed and thumbed through a copy of *National Geographic* while he waited. About ten minutes passed before a woman he vaguely recognized filed out of the office with a huff. She searched the reception area with a scowl on her face, but her anger melted away the instant she caught sight of Liam.

"Liam James, is that you? It's been forever." She rushed over and motioned for him to stand so she could wrap him in an awkward hug.

He pulled away and put a few feet between them. "I'm sorry. I'm not sure I remember meeting you before."

"Oh, you know me," the pretty redhead said, closing the gap by another foot or two. "It's Jackie Olson. I was one of the bridesmaids at your wedding. I heard what happened with Rebecca, by the way. I'm so sorry."

Olson. That made her the pastor's daughter. The red hair should have tipped him off.

"I'm so sorry I missed Rebecca's funeral. I wanted to come, but it was a long drive from Washington State where I was living at the time with my husband, but then . . . Well, we aren't together anymore. Hey, I suppose that means we're both single, you and me." She shrugged and offered a goofy smile that felt incredibly out of place.

Is she trying to flirt with me? This is not fun at all. How soon before I can get the heck out of Dodge?

Jackie carried on, undeterred by Liam's lack of response. "My husband, well, he didn't die, of course. Though truth be told, I kind of wish he had. That would make things so much easier. Just don't tell my dad I said that, or he'll be all over me making a case for what the scripture says." She heaved an exaggerated sigh. "Raising boys without their father is no small task, let me tell you. I feel like I'm here meeting with Principal Perkins every other day. Actually, I probably am here at least twice a week. I do hope things go better for you and your little girl. Molly, was it?"

Liam smiled to buy himself some time. *Which part of all that am I supposed to respond to?* Luckily, the principal appeared in the doorway and called for him to join her.

Jackie placed a conciliatory hand on his arm and gave him a meaningful look. "You go on back. I must be off myself, anyway. It was nice to see you, and if you need anything—and I do mean anything—at all, you give me a call. You promise you'll do that?"

"Um, sure."

"Good. I'll be seeing you soon, I'm sure." She leaned toward him for a moment, as if waiting for something. Another hug, maybe? Then Jackie offered another small wave and turned to walk away.

"Bye," he called before letting out a sigh of relief.

Hopefully this would be the last he saw of Jackie Olson for a while.

"Liam! I'm just going to grab a quick refresher on my coffee. Would you like me to pour you a cup?" Principal Perkins asked from her spot in the doorway.

"Sure, thanks."

"Go ahead and take a seat. I'll be with you a jiffy," she called, heading toward the back of the reception space and moving out of sight.

Liam turned back toward the waiting area to gather up his things, mostly paperwork pertaining to Molly's health and education to date. Before he could escape to the privacy of the principal's office, another townsperson descended upon him.

"Oh, hey there, stranger!" Dixon Cleary popped his head into the office, followed quickly by the rest of him. "Fancy meeting you here in a place we both rarely come. Unless you're enrolling Molly Sue?"

"Hi, Dixon." At least this person he knew and recognized. Dixon and his wife, Laura, had been trying to hire Liam to consult for their ranch almost as long as he'd been living in Sweet Grove. "What brings you here?"

"Oh, I'm just playing second fiddle to the missus today. We gave a presentation to the kids about the bees and making honey. I think they liked it, though I wish we could have gotten clearance to bring a hive or two with us. Say, have you thought some more about coming over to Honey Bee Hill? We've saved up for it and could use your business know-how, more for the cattle than the bees. What do you say?"

What *could* he say?

"Are you ready for me now?" Principal Perkins asked as she placed a Styrofoam cup of coffee in his hand.

"Ready as I'll ever be," he answered and turned back to the rancher briefly. "Dixon, let me finish up here, and then I'll head on out to see you at the ranch."

He sighed and took a long swig of coffee. He'd need all the energy he could get to make it through the rest of this day.

Jennifer had been given the rest of the day off to start her weekend early, partially to give her the time to digest her new work situation and partially because Patsy honestly didn't have the money to pay her.

No time like the present, she thought as she dragged her bike out from around the side of the apartment building and got ready to begin her search for the perfect new job. She'd start on the far end of town and work her way back home. By the end of the day, she would surely have a shiny new career to call her own. Right?

She pumped her legs hard, focusing on the rush as she took in deep lungfuls of air. No time to question things. She needed to act, to fix the problem before it became a problem at all. Jennifer preferred to think of setbacks like this one as opportunities instead of problems.

She had the *opportunity* to start an exciting new life in a town she loved with people she adored. That couldn't be so bad. Maybe she could be a waitress or a cook. Surely Kristina Rose and Jeffrey could use the extra help at the diner, given how busy it always was since Jeffrey had introduced the breakfast buffet. Then again, she wanted to make her own way, not rely on charity from friends. Maybe she'd end up running errands for city hall or cashing checks at the bank. Really, she could be or do anything so long as she kept an open mind.

She'd start with the ranches, which seemed like the best bet anyway. They were always hiring migrant workers for the busy seasons, so surely they had the budget to take on a new . . .

What in the hey would she do at a ranch? Milk cows? Mow grass? Well, she supposed she'd find out if they offered her the job. Besides, working with animals wouldn't be too different from working with kids.

Honey Bee Hill loomed on the horizon. It was the town's oldest and most well-established ranch, and while it was known for its award-winning Brahman cattle, Jennifer hoped to land a job helping with the tiny bee farm that also shared this space. Making honey would be something truly special! The news reports always talked about dwindling bee populations and the threat that posed. If Jennifer helped the bees, she'd be doing her small part to save the world, and what could be more perfect than that?

It took her nearly an hour to bike over to the ranch, even going as fast as she could. If she got the job, she'd probably have to drive the commute instead. Who knew what a ranch might pay? Maybe it would be enough to afford her expenses *and* get her car fixed, too. Wouldn't that be something?

She parked her bike up against a large maple tree and walked around back to see if she could catch one of the owners to discuss the prospect of her hire. As she rounded the small farm house, an endless field of purple and orange wildflowers came into view.

Wow. God's beauty at its finest.

A group of cows gazed in the distance, but the bee hives themselves were difficult to spot. Jennifer scanned the area. She'd come to the right ranch, hadn't she?

"Can I help you, miss?" a man called from the house's back wraparound porch.

She turned into the sun, holding her hand over her face like a visor. It took a moment for her eyes to focus, but when they did, she saw the ranch's owner, Dixon Clearly, sitting and having a chat with none other than Liam James!

Forget the hives. Now her heart was buzzing louder than all the bees in the world. "Howdy!" she called back, trying on ranch speak and liking the way it felt rolling off her tongue.

"Well, don't just stand there gawking. C'mere," Dixon said with a chuckle.

Liam smiled, too. Did that mean he was happy to see her? It certainly beat the frowns and scowls he'd worn through most of their previous meeting. She marched up to the porch, doing her best not to laugh at the sight of the two mismatched conversation partners. Dixon wore flannel and jeans along with work boots and a cap, while Liam sat dressed in an expensive-looking gray suit. She looked down at her own jeans, T-shirt, and sports shoes and figured she might indeed be a match for the ranch after all.

"What are you doing here?" Liam asked, rising to offer his seat once Jennifer had made it to the porch.

"I should ask you the same thing," she shot back. "Are you here for ranch business or for a fashion convention?" Despite her best attempts not to, she burst out in a rolling laugh.

Oops, now Liam's frown had returned.

SEVEN

All at once, Liam's day became far better and immeasurably worse. It was bad enough he'd been corralled into doing local consulting with the Clearys, but now the one woman he wanted to get off his mind was at the front and center once again.

Jennifer smiled shyly at him, almost as if she, too, had entertained more than a passing thought of him since their lunch on Sunday. He noted how natural and in her element she appeared in her simple jeans and cotton shirt ensemble. She could probably look at home in anything, at any place. He liked that about her. Her normally straight hair fell over her shoulders in soft waves, drawing focus toward her full lips and large smile.

He stared for a moment, unable to stop himself

from returning her grin. "What are you doing here?" he couldn't help but ask, unsure whether the surprise was welcome.

She mumbled something, but before she could finish, Jennifer erupted with laughter—not just a giggle or a chuckle, but a full-bellied, spurt-milk-from-your-nose kind of laugh.

And just like that, the romance of the moment evaporated into the crisp January air.

Dixon Cleary stood and clapped him on the back. "You are a bit overdressed, my friend."

"That's what this is about?" He gave Jennifer a stern look, the same kind of look he gave Molly Sue when she was acting out of turn.

"Sorry, sorry," Jennifer said between gasps for air, but still she laughed.

"Seems you could use a drink of water," Dixon said. "I'll just go fetch that from the kitchen, then." He disappeared around the side of the porch, leaving Jennifer and Liam on their own.

"So what? I'm wearing a suit," he explained. "I *am* here on business. What are you doing here?"

She stopped laughing and took a deep breath. "I'm here on business, too, actually."

"And that's what you wore? Maybe I should be the one laughing here." He added a conciliatory smile when he realized his words sounded far harsher than he'd intended. "I mean, you look beautiful, um, great. Uh, who's that on your shirt? I don't recognize that cat."

Jennifer looked down, her expression softening. "Oh, that's Pusheen. She's my favorite emoji. I have a pillow of her, too, back at home." She blushed, and he probably did, too, if the wave of heat surging through him was any indication. He'd called her beautiful—aloud—and while it was definitely true, it wasn't even close to appropriate.

Talk about something else, he told himself. *Anything else!*

"Ah," he said, wondering why he had an easier time talking to CEOs and other big business execs than to a woman he'd known for years. "It'll be another few years before I need to worry about texting and Facebook with Molly Sue. Right now, it's all Disney all the time."

"That's a good place to be," she answered, also appearing to be relieved by the topic change. "I love Disney."

"I would, too, if there were a bit less of it in my life," he admitted with a laugh.

"Nah, never let that magic go. The world needs more happily ever afters, don't you think?"

Yes, yes, I do. He thought of his own unhappy

ending, and all the words that had rushed to get out before died in his throat.

Dixon returned at that moment and handed Jennifer a tall glass of tap water.

"Thank you," she said before taking a long, deep gulp.

Dixon sank back into one of the porch chairs and set it rocking. "Now, what can I do you for, Miss Elliott?" he asked with a good-natured grin.

"Please." She set the empty glass down on the porch railing and waved her hand dismissively. "Only the kids call me 'Miss Elliott.' Besides, it would be weird if you did, considering I'm here to ask if you have any work available."

Oh no. What happened? Why would Jennifer need work all of a sudden? And why here of all places?

"Well . . ." Dixon began, but Liam had to ask, otherwise it would bother him all day, likely all week.

"At the ranch? But aren't you a daycare teacher?" Liam asked, realizing in that moment that Jennifer and Rebecca had both gone into the same profession though they focused on different age levels.

"I was and sort of still am, but Kitty Kids doesn't have enough work to go around at the moment, and I'm hoping that Honey Bee Hill does. So . . ." She shrugged and smiled. "What do you say, Dixon? Put me to work?"

Dixon stopped rocking and crossed one leg over the other. "Would that I could, but this just isn't our busy season. If you could come back in a few months, I'm sure I could find something for you to do, though."

Jennifer twisted her face in a strange expression— not sad but not happy either. "If I wait that long, I'll be asking to board with your cows," she said lightly but without an accompanying laugh. "Jonas Bryant is a fair landlord, but I can't just not pay him for several months on end."

Dixon stood and joined Jennifer and Liam near the railing. "Give me a few days. Let me talk to Laura. I'm sure we can rustle up something."

She shook her head adamantly and took a step back. "Oh no, you don't need to do that. I have a lot of places left to look, and I don't want to put you out, Dixon, really. Don't you worry about me. I'll find whatever work God wants me to have."

That was exactly the right line for a Sunday school teacher to deliver, yet somehow it didn't feel right coming from Jennifer. She didn't seem unhappy about her predicament, but Liam could not picture her doing anything but working with the kids she loved so dearly. And clearly they loved her back considering Molly Sue still found a way to mention Jennifer every single day since their lunch the past week.

Jennifer scratched at her shoulder and then trotted down the porch steps. "I should get going. I need to continue the hunt while we still have daylight. And I guess it's safe to assume that if it's offseason for you, it will be for the rest of the ranches, too. I guess I'll be heading back into town then. Thank you for hearing me out, Dixon. I'll see you another time, okay?"

"I mean what I said. Come back in a few days? The missus and I won't let you go hungry," Dixon offered one last time.

"I'll be fine. Don't you worry about me. See you in church this Sunday, right?" She waved, then turned and marched through the grass back toward the road.

"Jennifer, wait," Liam called, jogging after her. "Let me take you to lunch. Maybe I can help with the search."

She crossed her arms and kicked at the grass while she waited for him to catch up. "That's nice of you to offer," she said after a moment. "But this is something I need to do for myself."

Another stupid move on his part. Why was he always either too nice or too rude around Jennifer? No wonder she'd shot him down. He must be sending the most mixed-up signals in the history of stupid crushes.

Sweat beaded at his hairline despite the cool

temperature. "Oh yeah, of course, I didn't mean to suggest you couldn't—"

Jennifer uncrossed her arms and placed a hand on his forehead. "Relax, I know, and I appreciate the offer. Actually, you know what? There is something you can do if you don't mind."

"Of course!" Again with the overenthusiasm. *Do I sound too eager?*

"Could you drop me and my bike off at the library? It would save me a lot of time." She smiled at him and remained close as she waited for his answer. Part of him wanted to stall just to keep her near. He so rarely had any physical interaction with anyone other than goodnight hugs and kisses from Molly Sue, and this felt so much nicer than the onslaught from Jackie Olson had earlier that day. He liked Jennifer's smile, the sweet smell of freesia that clung to her T-shirt, the lilt of her words with just the slightest of Texas twangs.

All of it, he liked all of it. *All of her.*

How fitting they found themselves at a ranch at that moment, because suddenly Liam realized that there was no way around it. He was in deep cow pucky when it came to Jennifer Elliott.

* * *

Jennifer slid into Liam's immaculately kept car while he folded down the back seats and fit her bike in through the trunk. Her old, beat-up bike seemed glaringly out of place amid the posh interior.

"What kind of car is this?" she asked when he joined her upfront and shifted them into drive.

"Audi," he answered, keeping his focus on the road though there were no other cars anywhere nearby.

"Is it the same one you had when Rebecca . . . ?" She broke off before finishing the question. Even though Rebecca was often on her mind, especially when she spent even the smallest sliver of time with Liam, it still didn't feel natural or right to discuss her with him.

He winced and tightened his grip on the steering wheel. His nails matched the rest of him—clean and finely groomed.

She stared down at her own chewed-up nails, the remnants of glitter polish reminding her that Liam was a strong, put-together man, and she was far less settled in her own life.

"No, I got this one a few months ago. My lease was up," he explained with an apologetic shrug. Did he feel guilty about having a steady stream of one new luxury after the next when she didn't have a stable job?

It's okay, she wanted to say. *They're just things*. But she stopped herself when she realized that *things* were likely all Liam had—well, besides his adorable daughter, anyway. *Ah, Molly Sue,* the perfect topic to break the silence and keep her from saying anything else stupid and uncomfortable.

"Where's the kiddo today?" she asked. "I thought you homeschooled."

He tightened his grip on the steering wheel again as if doing so gave him strength. "We were homeschooling, but she starts at Sweet Grove Elementary on Monday. The tutor up and quit on us. It was a bit unexpected."

"You don't sound too happy about that, but I promise she'll love it at the school. The kids her age are all so sweet and a lot of fun, too. There's Josie, and Stephanie, and Mallory, and . . . Oh, Aiden Olson. That's Pastor Bernie's grandson."

"The little Olson's in second grade, too, huh?" He frowned.

"He's a bit of a troublemaker, but his heart is in the right place," Jennifer said, sticking up for the second newest member of her Sunday school class.

"It's not Aiden I'm worried about." The corners of his mouth hitched up in an aggravated smile. "I had a run in with Jackie earlier today, and suffice it to say, I'd rather avoid a repeat."

"Hey, be nice to Jackie. She's had a tough time lately. Did you know she had to move back to town because of a nasty divorce?"

"She mentioned that, and I promise you, I was perfectly nice. I just think she wanted me to be nice in a . . . in a *different* way."

"Oh . . . *Oh!*" So Jackie had made a play for Liam? That came as a bit of a shock seeing as she had every reason to swear off men for life. And Liam hadn't responded well. Did that mean he wasn't ready to date again or just that he wasn't interested in Jackie? How would he respond if Jennifer were to bat her eyelashes his way?

Neither said anything as they drove into town. A few minutes later, Liam parked in front of the library and turned toward Jennifer with a searching look on his face.

"Thanks for the ride," she mumbled, rushing to unlatch her seat belt and hop out of the car. "See you around!" She hoped Liam hadn't noticed the heat that had settled into her cheeks as she bolted out of his sight and into the security of the library.

Once inside, Jennifer ran up to the large circular desk at the center of the open room, then let out a deep breath she hadn't realized she'd been holding in.

She'd never been so happy to see the cranky librarian Sally Scott in all her life.

"What's the rush?" Sally hooked an eyebrow at Jennifer, then smiled just enough to show the slight gap between her two front teeth. "Did you run the whole way here?"

"What? No, of course not. I just wanted to talk with you real quick."

"So talk," Sally snipped at her. "Are you looking for a book?"

"No, I'm actually looking for work. Do you need a librarian's aid, an administrative assistant, a story time reader?" Jennifer placed her hands flat on the desk to stop herself from nervously chewing on her fingernails. "Literally anything, anything at all?"

Sally tapped a pen on the edge of her spiral-bound notebook, appearing to think the request over, which was more than Jennifer had expected from the town crab. She remained calm and pensive as always, and Jennifer wondered for a moment whether something was broken when it came to the librarian's emotional receptors—or perhaps her heart.

"No," Sally said after a moment. "There's hardly enough work to keep me busy, let alone a new hire."

"Okay. Well, thanks for trying," Jennifer said and turned to leave.

"Hey," Sally called after her, her voice more

expressive than usual. "You're not exactly the librarian type. You're way too bubbly."

Jennifer tensed. Had Sally just called her back to insult her? It was probably for the best that they had no work for her here. Having to put up with mean old Sally all week would drive her to an early grave.

Sally continued despite Jennifer's growing agitation. "You're a teacher, right?" The flatness returning to her voice. "Have you tried asking about substitute work with the school district? I would start there, I mean, if *I* were you."

"That's actually not a bad idea," Jennifer admitted. "I'll just bike out there and see. If I hurry, I should be able to make it before school lets out for the day."

"Good luck." Sally opened her notebook and returned to her work as Jennifer bolted back out through the double doors. Maybe mean old Sally wasn't so bad after all. Jennifer would have to come back to thank her if this suggestion bore fruit. Maybe she could invite her to the group's next karaoke night, convince everyone to give her a chance.

As for Jennifer, teaching had always been her calling. Maybe she'd find deeper fulfillment working with the older grades. This unwanted layoff really could be part of God's plan, lead to an even happier life. All she needed to do was ask the right person for a new opportunity. She'd start at the elementary school and work her way up to the middle school and the high school. Luckily, all of Sweet Grove's schools sat near one another on the far end of Main Street.

Unluckily, she couldn't find her bike anywhere. A moment later, she remembered loading it into Liam's car back at the ranch. She'd taken off in such a hurry, they'd forgotten to unload it.

Looked like she'd be walking home.

Crud.

EIGHT

L iam watched as Jennifer flew from his car as fast as her feet could carry her. Why had he gone on and on about Jackie Olson? Jennifer probably thought it was his way of warning her off, of telling her that he wasn't ready for a relationship. But he wasn't, was he?

He sighed and began the long drive home, mentally berating himself as he drove. Though the opportunity hadn't really presented itself, he'd thought about asking Jennifer if she might be interested in working as a tutor for Molly Sue as she made the transition from homeschooling to public school. His daughter would need the extra guidance to catch up with her classmates. Jennifer needed the work, and if he was being honest with himself, he wanted the chance to see her more often, to add some structure to their relationship, whatever it was, whatever it could turn into.

But, no, he hadn't asked about that. Instead, he'd more or less told her that the idea of flirting revolted him to the core. Unfortunately, from the look on Jennifer's face when he'd relayed his encounter with Jackie Olson, she'd received his message loud and clear.

He'd have to face her again that Sunday when he picked Molly Sue up from Sunday school, but until then, he'd do his best to catch up on work and—if any time remained after that—try to enjoy his weekend.

In the grand scheme of things, none of this mattered. So he had a crush? It didn't mean anything, couldn't mean anything. He was still a married man, end of story.

Liam let out a long sigh and turned on the radio, willing the music to wash over his brain and cleanse his thoughts away. He didn't bother to change the station from Molly's favorite pop music. Truth be told, he didn't have anything to change it to. It had been a long time since he'd enjoyed music, since he'd enjoyed much of anything, really. These days, every love song reminded him of what he lost, and most of the time he tried to tune out whatever Disney song

Molly Sue had insisted they listen to for the umpteenth time.

The tinkling of piano keys introduced a slow love ballad that danced into the car, and he slammed the radio off, choosing instead to drive the rest of the way in silence.

At home, Molly Sue and her tutor, Megan, ran around the front yard in a game of chase. The moment he put his car in park, Molly Sue ran up to him and tapped on the window. He rolled it down so she could give him a big, wet kiss on the cheek.

"I thought you'd never come back!" she cried, her cheeks red, much as Jennifer's had been before she disappeared into the library.

"I'll always come back." He gave his girl a smile, one he meant from the bottom of his heart. "Give me a second to settle things up with Megan, and then I'll be in, okay?"

"Okay, Daddy." Molly Sue's eyes grew wide as she peeked into the back of the car. "Oh! Are we going to ride bikes when you're done talking to Miss Megan?"

"What? I mean, I guess we could, but—"

"That bike is too big for me, so that means it's for you, right? But why is it purple?" She gestured toward the back seat, and that was when Liam finally remembered. Jennifer had taken off in such a hurry that she had forgotten her bike. Awkward or not, he'd need to return it to her—and he'd need to do it now.

Megan came over and stood beside Molly Sue in the driveway, a stack of school materials held against her chest, purse slung over her shoulder.

"I am so sorry," he told her. "I forgot something important back in town. Can you stay with Molly Sue for an extra hour? I'll add to your pay. I just have to . . ."

"Yeah, no problem," she answered much to his relief. "I don't have anywhere to be. Take your time."

"Thank you," he said to Megan. He turned back to Molly Sue. "I'll be back soon. I have to take this bike back to its owner. If you want to ride bikes, I'll order one for me online, and we can go for a ride together next weekend, okay?"

His daughter's eyes danced with mischief as she studied the bike laying forgotten in the back seat. "It's Miss Elliott's, isn't it?"

"How did you . . . ? Yes, and I need to get it back to her. I'll be home in an hour."

As he pulled back out of his drive, he wondered how on earth Molly Sue could have guessed the bike belonged to Jennifer—and even more so, why she was so happy about it.

* * *

Molly Sue and Rebecca
Fourteen months ago

Molly Sue counted up her Halloween candy. She definitely had more this year than any year before! It helped that Daddy had dressed her bicycle up like a unicorn to match her princess costume and to help them reach more houses faster while trick-or-treating the night before. She loved her unicorn bike and didn't think she would ever take the special dressing off. Swooping down their steep driveway was even more fun when the shiny white streamers that made up the unicorn's mane floated in the wind.

Now if only her bike could fly, too, like Princess Sofia's flying horse friend, Minimus. That would be the very best thing in the world! If her bike could fly, then she could go visit Mommy in Heaven anytime she wanted!

"Molly Sue, don't you think you've had enough candy?" her mother said as she shuffled through the kitchen and went to get some water from the fridge. "If you eat too much, your tummy will hurt. And it will serve you right, too."

"One more?" she asked with a huge toothy grin she knew her mother would not be able to resist. "Please?"

"If you think it's worth the risk. But tummy ache or no tummy ache, you'll still need to finish your school work for the day, so choose wisely." Mommy arched an eyebrow before taking a long, slow drink from her glass.

Molly Sue decided it was worth the risk. She hadn't eaten any of her peanut butter cups yet, and—oh my gosh—she would love to have the taste of chocolate and peanuts in her mouth until dinnertime instead of the icky yellow Starburst she'd eaten just before her mother had come back downstairs.

She tore the orange wrapper from her candy and popped the whole thing into her mouth. So yummy!

Her mother laughed. "For both our sakes, I hope your stomach can handle that giant influx of sugar. Now come over to the table. I have something very important to teach you today."

Molly trotted over and took a seat.

"Good," her mom said with a smile. "Now we need to work on your reading."

"But I already know how to read."

"Yes, and you are doing a great job, too, but I need you to work hard on getting even better. Can you do that for me?"

Molly Sue nodded and watched as her mother uncapped a pen and wrote big loopy letters on a piece of paper. "What does this say?"

"It says my name, Molly Sue!" She loved seeing her name written out on paper. It was one of her most favorite things. "But you wrote the S wrong, Mommy."

"This is cursive," Mommy explained as she wrote out Molly Sue's name again right below the first one. "Isn't it pretty?"

"I guess, but why can't you just write the normal way?"

"I want you to learn both ways." She stopped writing and looked up at Molly Sue, then winked. "You know, just in case. Now look here. What does this one say?"

"L love you?" Molly Sue guessed, even though it didn't make much sense.

"Very close. That big *L* is actually an *I*. Some of the cursive letters look a little different, but many of them look the same. You're doing a really good job, especially since this is our first cursive lesson."

Her mother wrote both the sentences again, putting them together: *I love you, Molly Sue.*

"That says, 'I love you, Molly Sue.' I still think that *S* looks silly, though."

Mommy laughed and shook her head. "You know what? You're right. You'll get used to it though, I promise. And hey, Molly Sue?"

"Yeah?" she asked as she pulled a piece of purple

construction paper from across the table and uncapped a big blue marker. She wanted to try writing the silly *S*, too.

Mommy guided Molly Sue's hand across the paper. "Would it be okay if I kept writing to you like this?"

She nodded as she continued dragging her marker in big, slow loops. "As part of school?"

Mommy nodded, too. "Yes, but I also have some very important instructions for you, and I don't want either of us to forget, so I am going to write them down, okay?"

"Is this part of me being Daddy's angel?"

"Yes, it is. You are so smart. I knew you were the perfect person for the job."

"A job?" This was the first time Mommy had called being an angel a job, and she wasn't sure she wanted a job. Jobs seemed like things you didn't like to do, things you had to do instead of playing. Kids weren't supposed to have jobs. She decided to ask her mommy about this in a nice way to make sure she understood right. "A job like Daddy has?"

"Kind of. Molly Sue, I know you are still little, but I'm going to talk to you like a grown-up. Is that okay?" She waited for Molly to nod before going on. "I want to explain to you a little bit more about jobs, since you have one of your own now. That's right, being Daddy's angel. It's kind of a job, but it's not the same as Daddy's job. You see, some people work to make enough money to eat and have a house and buy the things they want. Others work because they are trying to get away from something."

This made Molly Sue feel sad deep in her heart. She pictured her heart like the Grinch's but instead of growing two sizes, it broke in half. "Daddy works a lot. Does that mean he is trying to get away from us?"

"Not at all, sweetie. Come sit on my lap while I tell you the rest."

Molly Sue climbed up slowly, careful not to hurt Mommy as she settled in. She then played with the sapphire pendant on her mother's neck as she listened.

"Daddy is very good at his job, but you're right. He's also using it to get away—not from you or me— but from the sadness he feels. It's kind of like how some people eat extra candy when they feel sad."

Molly Sue felt embarrassed as she thought about her decision to eat an extra piece of candy despite her mother's warning. "I didn't know I was eating candy because I feel sad. I'm sorry. I don't think I'm sad all the time, but I *do* feel sad that you have to go to Heaven."

"And Daddy does, too, so he spends extra time

working to try not to think about that, to try not to feel sad."

Molly Sue thought hard about that before asking, "But won't you still have to go to Heaven anyway even if Daddy does do all that extra work?"

"Yes, and you're very smart to understand that. It's actually part of your job as Daddy's angel." Mommy took a few deep breaths. She seemed tired, like maybe she needed a nap.

And even though her mother had just said she was smart, Molly Sue struggled to understand. "To do extra work?"

"No, your job will be easy, but also very important. After I go, I know your daddy is going to work even harder to try to forget how much he misses me. Your job is different. It's not like Daddy's. I need you to pay attention to how much time Daddy spends working at his job and how sad he looks, too. If he's working too much or looks too sad, then you'll need to help him extra."

"But how will I know if he's very extra sad or just the usual sad?" Molly asked, unable to find the answer on her own.

"That's a good question. I'm still thinking about that myself, but that's also what the letters I plan to write you are about. Now let's work some more on our *S*'s, okay?"

* * *

How could Jennifer have been so stupid to forget her bike in the back of Liam's car like that? Very, very stupid, all right. She didn't have his number to call and ask for him to bring it back, and she couldn't be sure he'd show up for church that Sunday. So where did that leave her, and what was she going to do?

She jogged back home, willing the pounding pulse in her ears to drown out her angry, nagging thoughts. First, she'd at least call the schools to ask about any substitute opportunities, then she'd take a long, luxurious bath—with bubbles, lots of bubbles.

She quickened her gait to a run, looking forward to the bath that awaited her back at home. She'd saved the unicorn bath bomb Maisie had given her as part of her Christmas gift, and this would be the perfect opportunity to put it to use.

Once home, she booted up her computer and scrolled through Facebook, making sure to like the pictures her sister had posted earlier that day, and then looked up the number for the main school district office.

"You've got this," she told herself, wondering why she felt so nervous about making such a routine call.

"Yes, we'd be happy to add you to the substitute

teaching list, Jennifer," the friendly administrator responded. "Can you e-mail us your resume and references so we can officially add you to the system?"

"I sure can! This is great. When should I expect to receive my first assignment?" Finally, her day had begun to turn around, and it was all because of Sally Scott. Who would have thought?

The woman on the other end of the line hesitated. "We *can* add you to the list, but this is a small school district and not a lot of opportunities come up. Please don't count on this too much."

"But you will add me, right?" Jennifer asked, trying not to let defeat creep in.

"Of course. I gave you the e-mail address, right?"

"Yes, thank you. I'll send it later tonight," she responded, hoping her voice still sounded chipper and, moreover, hirable.

When they hung up, Jennifer headed straight to the bathroom. She'd send her resume along later, but if there was no hurry, then there was no point in rushing either. That morning, she had been so sure that she'd have a new job in hand by the end of the day, yet had nothing to show for it now that she'd done the work of putting herself out there.

Maybe she *would* need to beg her friends for help, after all.

Okay, so that wasn't her first choice, but she'd save

collecting charity as her final option. Maybe she'd find something tomorrow, or maybe she'd end up working with a friend and end up finding her perfect fit that way.

The Lord worked in mysterious ways, but he also had her back. She needed to have faith, and more than that, patience. After all, it was a virtue, and one she often forgot to exercise.

For now, though, she had a tub of hot water and a sparkly pink, yellow, green, and purple bath bomb. She'd never tried one of these before and was really looking forward to it, especially since there was a prize hidden inside.

She settled in, then unwrapped the soapy, scented goodness and placed it in the water at her knees. It exploded in a blooming cloud of color and sparkle. The bubbles tickled and the aroma of lavender and citrus, while an unusual combo, was absolutely lovely.

Nope, this wasn't such a bad way to end the day. She could put her struggles behind her and go to bed relaxed, happy, and ready for whatever the weekend would bring. And as soon as she could afford it, she'd definitely be purchasing more of these bombs, she thought as she fished a clear plastic container out of the water and popped it open to find a cute silver ring with a light blue gem at its center.

That, of course, was when the doorbell buzzed.

But I'm not expecting anyone, she reminded herself, relaxing back into the tub and flexing her toes. *Must be for the neighbors. They probably hit my button by accident.*

Buzz! Buzz!

Someone else will get it. She closed her eyes and took a deep breath, taking in all the delicious smells and letting out all the worries that had stacked up during the day.

The buzzing seemed to have stopped. *Good riddance,* she thought, splashing gently in the water and amusing herself with how the colors swirled and rearranged themselves with each disruption.

A series of knocks then sounded at her door. *What the heck?*

"Who is it?" she called, trying to mask the frustration in her voice.

"It's Liam," the muffled answer came.

Liam? She looked down at the sheath of bubbles that hid her naked body. *No, no, no.*

"Um, just a sec!" She stumbled to her feet, sloshing water everywhere in the process, then grabbed her bathrobe from the nearby hook and wrapped it around her body.

A quick glance down at her still slippery body confirmed that the robe was far too short to be considered decent for company. *When I have money,*

I'm going to buy a big granny moo-moo, just in case this ever happens again, she promised herself before swinging open the door to greet her unexpected guest.

Liam's eyes bulged as he took in the sight of her, bare legs and all. Thankfully, she had shaved just a couple of days back, so the stubble shouldn't have been visible unless he was really looking for it. Somehow Jennifer doubted that.

She felt flushed all over, but at least she could blame it on the heat from her bath this time. "What are you doing here?" she demanded, perhaps a bit harsher than she'd wanted to come across.

"I . . . uh . . . Do you w-want to get dressed first?" He looked away back toward the stairs and smiled.

"Oh, so you're enjoying this, are you?" she huffed.

"Maybe a little," he admitted. "Go put on some clothes, and then I'll tell you why I'm here." He still didn't look at her, and she wondered if he was just being a gentleman or if he truly had no interest in seeing how she looked under all her jeans and T-shirts.

Well, he didn't have to tell her twice—um, make that three times. "I'll be right back." She clutched her robe to her chest to ensure the situation didn't go from bad to much, much worse and headed toward her room.

She could have sworn she heard Liam laughing to himself as she went. So much for not being awkward around him. It seemed no matter the time, the place, or the circumstance, she could always count on finding new ways to embarrass herself.

But wasn't that just the rule when it came to crushes?

NINE

L iam needed a distraction, and a good one, too, if he was going to wipe the image of beautiful Jennifer from his mind. Why was God testing him like this? Wasn't it enough that He'd taken Rebecca from him? Or that He'd sat back on his cloud and watched as Liam made a mess of things both at lunch last week and in the car with Jennifer?

And now to stumble upon her undressed on top of everything? It seemed God enjoyed making jokes at Liam James's expense.

Better comedy than tragedy, he reasoned.

Liam laughed to himself as he glanced around Jennifer's living room, taking in the old box monitor on the desk jammed into the corner by the window. On the opposite side of the room stood a tall bookshelf, every inch of space crammed with picture frames, knickknacks, and few actual books.

He picked up a framed photo of Jennifer and her friends at their high school graduation, the girls leaned in tight for a hug. Rebecca, who had returned from college expressly for the occasion, stood next to Jennifer, and both wore equally huge smiles on their faces. Rebecca had been dark-haired and fair-skinned, tall, and curvy, while Jennifer was short, lean, and blonde. They looked so physically different from each other, everything except for their piercing blue eyes and the happiness they both wore splashed across their beautiful faces.

And they were beautiful—*both of them*—his past and his future arm in arm beaming up at him from the comfort of a worn wood frame. *Wait, did I just . . . ?*

He needed to stop thinking of Jennifer this way, as if she already belonged to him. At some point, he'd forgotten what it was like to be a man simply interested in a woman. No promises, no rings. Just pure attraction.

He'd been committed to Rebecca years before her death. He didn't know how to show casual interest, didn't know how to go anywhere but all the way. Had he somehow already decided that he loved Jennifer? And if so, how? It had been less than a week since he noticed the strange new feelings take root, and already he was ready to plant a garden, put up a canopy, and marry her under it.

That is, if he could talk to her without saying the wrong darned thing every single time. He needed to stop this madness. He was married to Rebecca, whether or not she was still around to return his commitment. He owed her his loyalty.

And yet, Jennifer made him feel the first whispers of happiness he'd felt in a very long time. Molly Sue adored her, too, and Jennifer had a problem that he could actually help solve—and by doing so, help himself in the process. What if God wasn't toying with him at all? What if this was all part of His larger plan?

Liam paced the small room, trying to figure out what it was he wanted when it came to Jennifer. Heck, when it came to life as a whole.

He needed to return her bike, that was the first thing. He could do that; that part was easy. But after that?

Was it hot in here? It felt hot. He removed his suit jacket and unbuttoned his collar. Still too hot.

"Do you mind if I pour myself a glass of water?" he called. How long had she been in there? It felt like forever.

"Go for it," she answered from behind the closed door.

Liam stalked into the kitchen. His eyes immediately landed on the fridge, which acted as a canvas for a variety of colorful artworks. There, among them, was the picture his Molly Sue had drawn for her during their lunch at Ernie's. The reds, greens, and blues swirled into an angel —an angel his daughter had said was her mother.

He reached out to stroke the portrait, feeling the sting of loss as fresh as ever.

"It's a beautiful drawing," Jennifer said, coming up behind him and studying the picture alongside him. "It reminds me of how Rebecca always had a smile on her face, even during those last days. She always rose above. Just like in this picture."

Liam felt the beginnings of tears well up behind his eyes. He would not cry, could not cry.

"I miss her, too," Jennifer whispered. "I think of her every day."

They stood in silence. She seemed to be giving him his space until he was ready to speak first. When he finally turned toward her, he noticed that she, too, had tears shining in her eyes.

"I-is it okay to talk about her?" she asked after a moment's hesitation.

"It's so hard," he confessed. "When I think about

the bad times, I get angry at how unfair it is that she was taken away. And when I remember the good times, I think about the fact that we'll never have them again. And I guess I worry that I'll forget them in time, that I'll forget her."

"Liam, no." She grabbed his arm and forced him to look at her. A stern expression crossed her face. "You'll never forget her. Neither will I. She was a very special person, my best friend."

"I know you loved her, too," he replied. Her hand stayed on his arm. They remained close, his breaths syncing with hers. "I think maybe that's why Molly Sue likes you so much, and why I like you, too."

She smiled sadly and looked toward the tiled floor, letting go of his arm as she did. He felt a sudden rush of coldness as they moved apart.

"Did you . . . did you get the glass of water you needed?" She paced toward the cabinets and grabbed a glass before he could answer and returned a moment later handing him a polka-dotted tumbler full of water.

He accepted the glass but didn't voice his thanks, instead choosing to offer her a pert nod. He was just so tired in that moment.

Jennifer took a deep breath. "So what brings you by?"

Oh, right. He had a reason, though he'd forgotten

it the moment he laid eyes on Molly Sue's drawing. "I accidentally drove off with your bike."

"Yes, I noticed." She returned to the sink and poured herself a glass of water, too. "Thank you for bringing it back. You did bring it back, didn't you?"

"I did."

"Thank you," she repeated, passing her glass from one hand to the other and back as he took a quick drink from his. She appeared to be lost in thought, which gave him the perfect opportunity to look at her, truly look at her. Her wet hair had been slicked back away from her cheeks and tucked behind her ears. Not a trace of makeup lined her face. She wore jeans as she usually did, and a lace-lined tank top instead of a T-shirt. Her cheeks appeared red and rosy, likely from the tears they had shared only moments before. Above it all, though, she was beautiful, natural, angelic—just like the Rebecca in his daughter's portrait.

He couldn't help but wonder yet again if God had sent Jennifer to him and Molly Sue for a reason.

She took his glass from him and returned both tumblers to the sink. "Was there something else, Liam?"

"Yes," he found himself saying. "I'd like to offer you a job."

She took a step back and shook her head. "A job?"

The hitch in her voice suggested she was nearly as surprised as he was by this sudden offer.

"A job," he confirmed. "That is, if you still need one."

"Well, yeah. Things at the library didn't exactly go as planned." Her laugh eased the tension that had built between them.

Yes, this is right.

"Remember how I told you Molly Sue is starting at the elementary school next week? Well, she's been homeschooled for over a year now, and I think she could use some extra help from someone she knows and likes and who also happens to have a degree in education."

"A private tutor for Molly Sue?" Jennifer blinked up at him, her expression unreadable. Had he acted out of turn yet again?

"It was just an idea," he fumbled. "Don't feel obligated. I just thought maybe—"

"Liam," she cut him off. "That would be perfect, actually. Tell me more."

* * *

Sunday, beautiful Sunday! Jennifer woke up feeling much better than she had the day before. Most of Saturday had been spent driving around town and picking up supplies for her science lessons with Molly Sue, all while praying her car wouldn't break down in the process.

She studied her closet, settling on a nice shirt and skirt combo for that morning's service. Today she'd be talking to the children about charity and doing unto others. She even planned to give them a homework assignment to find one person to help in an unexpected way that week. She loved doing her part to make Sweet Grove a nice place to live.

When she arrived at the First Street Church, she found her friends already gathered in the foyer gossiping among themselves.

"Hey, cutie!" Elise called. "About time you showed up."

Jennifer checked her dumb phone and stuck out her tongue. "Hey, I'm still fifteen minutes early. Cut me some slack, blondie."

Everyone laughed as Jennifer gave out hugs.

"How was yesterday?" Maisie asked as she worried her lip. After the embarrassing incident with Liam the night before, Jennifer had called to clue her friend in on her new money troubles. "Did you find something?"

"Wait, what's going on?" Kristina Rose asked.

"Are you keeping something from us?" Elise added.

Summer stayed quiet but reached for Jennifer's hand and gave it a supportive squeeze.

"Yeah, I kind of lost my job at Kitty Kids this Friday," she confessed.

"What? That's insane! I'll march right in there and give Patsy a piece of my mind. She's crazy to let you go." Elise didn't need much encouragement to go to war on her friends' behalf. She often ended up as the protector of the group even when there wasn't actually anything to protect them from.

"Stop," Maisie said, placing an arm in front of Elise's chest before she could zoom off in search of Patsy and make things far worse for everyone, especially Jennifer. "Patsy didn't do anything wrong. She really tried to make things work, but money is tight. Besides, you're still part-time there. Right, Jennifer?"

Jennifer nodded.

Kristina Rose offered her another hug. Jennifer couldn't believe how small her friend felt in her arms. She had lost so much weight so quickly, even her face had begun to change. "Do you need to pick up some shifts at the diner?" Kristina asked. "Let me and Jeffrey help until you're back on your feet."

Jennifer laced her fingers and stretched her palms out in front of her, trying to act casual as she made her big reveal. "Actually, I've already found another job to make ends meet."

"Oh?" Maisie asked. "You didn't tell me that."

"It happened kind of suddenly."

"Well, spill it!" Elise spat. "Don't keep us in suspense here."

I have no reason to be embarrassed, so why am I acting like this? Jennifer flushed. "I'll be doing some afterschool tutoring for Molly Sue James," she mumbled.

"Molly Sue? Isn't she homeschooled?" Summer asked.

"She was, but she's starting at the elementary school next week and needs some help adjusting."

"They found the perfect person for the job." Maisie beamed at her. "Congratulations. I can't believe how quickly you found a new position!"

"I can," Elise added. "Jennifer is awesome. Of course Liam snapped her right up."

"Oh, *Liam.* That's right," Kristina Rose whispered. "I saw you two talking at the grand reopening of our restaurant. Is he doing okay?"

"Hey!" Elise interjected once more. "Something going on that we should know about there, Jenn?"

Jennifer felt her throat tighten. No words would be getting out to confirm or deny that one.

"Stop it," Maisie said, slugging Elise in the arm. "This is about work, not dating. Liam's still mourning Rebecca. You *know* that."

"You're right," Elise said. "I shouldn't have gone there. Besides, Liam isn't your type anyway. Is he, Jenn?"

"Um, guys, the service is starting," Summer said. "I'm going to go find Ben. Catch you all later?"

"Oh, you can be sure of it," Elise promised before linking arms with Kristina Rose and disappearing into the sanctuary, Maisie following close behind.

TEN

Liam and Molly Sue had gone shopping that weekend, and today they showed up in their Sunday finest, primped and pressed and fresh off the rack. Molly Sue had chatted excitedly the entire drive into town, and Liam couldn't help but share in her happiness, too.

The talk he'd had with Jennifer standing by her fridge, his decision to offer her a job, and *her* decision to accept—they all put him at ease, convinced him that this had been God's plan all along. He'd brought Jennifer back into their lives to help Molly Sue move forward with hers, to rejoin school, make friends. The bubbly Sunday school teacher had reentered their lives at exactly the right moment, too—or rather, they'd reentered hers.

It wasn't about love, not at all. God just needed a way to get Liam's attention, and now that He had it, everything would be just fine.

"Good morning," he said when he returned to pick up Molly Sue after the service.

"Hi, Liam. Good to see you both again," Jennifer responded with a polite smile.

"Well, goodbye," Liam said, turning to head back toward the parking lot.

Molly Sue had other ideas, though. She let go of his hand, crossed her arms, and refused to budge.

Liam turned back toward her and found her wearing an exaggerated smile despite her angry posture. "That was a really good lesson, Miss Elliott," she told Jennifer loudly. "Will you come to lunch with us so I can ask you a few follow-up questions?"

Liam was absolutely certain his little girl had lifted those words directly from a phone call he'd had with a client the previous week. He couldn't help but chuckle despite his discomfort.

Jennifer kneeled down to meet Molly Sue face to face. "And what questions did you have?"

Molly Sue scratched her chin in thought, then gestured wide. "I have so many questions. So, so many questions. That's why I want you to come to lunch with us." She turned back toward Liam and gave him an animated wink, scrunching up the whole left side of her face as part of the gesture.

Oh, she's definitely up to something. Which of her Disney movies is she trying to bring to life now?

"I'm sorry, sweetie," Jennifer answered, tucking one of Molly's stray curls back behind her ear. "I already have plans for lunch today, but I'll see you tomorrow after your first day of school, and we'll have our special tutoring session. I'm really excited about that. Aren't you?"

Molly Sue shrugged. "I guess."

"Hey, kiddo," Elise said, swooping into the classroom. "Why don't you and your dad come with? A bunch of us are headed to Mabel's for Jeffrey's famous brunch buffet. We can easily squeeze in two more. What do you say?"

Liam watched as the youth pastor winked at her friend, much the same way Molly Sue had just winked at him. When would these two have gotten a chance to come together, and what on earth could they have joined forces to concoct?

"I don't think so," he said at the same time that his daughter turned to him and said, "Oh, Daddy, can we? *Please?*"

Well, now I'm stucker than stuck. "Is that okay with you?" he asked Jennifer.

Jennifer smiled and nodded gently.

"Of course it is," Elise answered for her. "And hey, Molly Sue, I want you to sit right next to me. Would you like that?"

Molly Sue bobbed her head and placed her hand into Elise's. "Can I ride with you?"

Elise looked to Liam for approval. "Go ahead," he said with a sigh.

And even though he left straightaway, somehow only one seat was left when he reached the restaurant, and it was right beside Jennifer Elliott.

"Do you mind if I sit?" He had to raise his voice to be heard over the noisy gathering of more than twenty diners crowded together in the middle of the restaurant.

Jennifer pulled the chair back and patted the seat. "You seem a bit out of sorts," she pointed out once he'd scooted himself back up to the table.

"What? No. I'm just not exactly used to big crowds. Normally it's just me and my computer, or me and Molly Sue." He glanced around the busy restaurant. Almost as many people had come here as had attended the morning service. Turning back toward Jennifer, he asked, "Is the whole town here or what? It's almost as busy as it was on the grand reopening."

"Ah, so you *do* remember that."

He unwrapped his silverware bundle so that he'd

have something to do with his hands. "Yes, I believe you showed up in your prom dress?" He felt the smile rise from out to the corners of his face and didn't try to stop it.

Jennifer proudly agreed with his recollection. "And I believe you stood by the door and scowled at everyone, then left early?"

"Touché." He chuckled and set his fork and knife down neatly in front of him.

"How long has it been since you've seen everybody?" she asked so softly he almost couldn't make out the words amid all the other conversations taking place around them.

"The funeral mostly, but it's been at least twice as long since I've felt like a normal person around them. I never got to know everyone outside of being Rebecca's husband, and now that she's gone . . ."

"You're still Rebecca's husband, but you're also yourself. Don't sit here talking to me all afternoon. Use this opportunity to reintroduce yourself. Everyone has missed you and Molly Sue, and we're happy to have you back."

"I wouldn't know where to begin," he admitted.

"Begin with Ben and Summer." She leaned in close and whispered to him, her breath tickling his ear. He liked having her near. He liked it a lot, way too much for her to only be a teacher or a friend. Was

God testing him? If so, what did he have to do to pass?

"They're getting married this spring, and I can guarantee you'll be invited." With each soft syllable, a new wave of heat coursed through Liam's whole body. "Besides, Summer is new to town, and you're basically starting over yourself. That's something you have in common."

He wanted to turn to face her, but moving his head even slightly would put them in kissing range, and God hadn't sent her as a marriage prospect. *You haven't, have you?* he asked God silently. *Could you please just stop already? This is getting too hard to ignore, and Molly Sue needs her help. Take these feelings from me, oh God.*

"What do I say?" he asked, drawing his gaze down the table until it landed on Ben and his future wife, who were seated at the far end.

Jennifer let out a snort. "Congratulate them on their engagement, duh."

"And then what?" He continued to glance around the restaurant until he found Molly Sue deep in conversation with Elise and some of the other local women. She caught his attention and gave him a huge thumbs-up.

Luckily, Jennifer was too busy giving him instructions to notice. "Then Summer will have loads to say, and you won't need to say another word unless you want to. Once you start the conversation, people won't be so hesitant to come up to you and talk. Right now, they're nervous and don't know what to say."

"Well, that makes . . ." He quickly counted up their dining partners. "Twenty-three of us, then."

She laughed. "Look, here are the high points to get you through lunch. Mabel retired and left the restaurant to Jeffrey, who invited Kristina Rose to be his partner. They're dating, but not engaged. And Kristina Rose had gastric bypass surgery in the fall and has lost about eighty pounds and counting. Susan Davis has been sober going on four months now following her stay in rehab, and we're all really proud of her. Iris Smith took her dream vacation this summer and came back to hear endless horror stories about the adventures her little parrot Sunny Sunshine had in her absence." She went down the table, sharing little tidbits about each of their neighbors' lives, then ended with, "And Elise is up to something, but that's nothing new."

Liam looked at each person as Jennifer shared their latest news but avoided meeting Molly Sue's eyes again since Jennifer was obviously paying attention now and would catch any silly encouragements his daughter decided to send his way. "And I'm supposed to remember all that *how*?"

"Just go talk to Summer and Ben. The rest will come back to you when you need it, and if you need a refresher, I'm right here. Now go." She gave him a nudge and reassuring smile, and just like that, he was off to talk with his neighbors and learn about all the pieces of their lives he had missed during the past couple of years.

Seemed Molly Sue wasn't the only James family member who would be reintegrating with the town this week. Still, as nice as it was feeling like he had somewhere to belong again, Liam would have much rather spent the entire meal glued to Jennifer's side.

* * *

Jennifer struggled to breathe beneath the weight of Patsy's giant hug.

"You give that Liam a big kiss from all of us at Kitty Kids," Patsy insisted. "This worked out perfectly, and after I'd worried over it so long!"

Jennifer put her hands on each of Patsy's shoulders to create a barrier. One more giant hug and she'd be flat as a pancake. "I'm just happy I get to stay on in the mornings. I would've missed the little boogers too much if I'd had to leave altogether."

Patsy cocked her head back in a laugh. "And I'd have gone crazy with no other grown-ups around."

Jennifer's eyes darted from one cat decoration to the next, wondering if perhaps her employer had already gone just a little bit crazy on her own.

Other than the excessive hugs, Jennifer's morning played out exactly as it always had for the last few years. Around lunch time, though, she walked home to prepare for her first lesson with Molly Sue later that afternoon. *Maybe Molly would like a healthy snack to tide her over before the learning started.* Liam was certainly paying her enough to afford to do something a little extra, and she needed to make a run to Sweet Grove Market besides.

"Please Lord, give my car the strength to make it there and back," she prayed as she jammed her key into the ignition. The drive was a short one, but she trusted her old coupe less and less each time she got behind the wheel, especially since the winter chill had begun to set in.

She and the car both made it to the grocery store in one piece, and for that, she was thankful. After a couple of months of tutoring Molly Sue, she could easily sock away enough to fix her stupid car once and for all. That is, if Liam actually needed her for that long. Molly was a smart kid. What if she learned everything she needed in just a few weeks? Then where would that leave Jennifer?

"Back to square one," she muttered to herself as she grabbed a cart from the corral and pushed her way into the store.

"Hey, Ben!" She waved to her friend who was stocking shelves in the instant foods aisle. "Is Maisie in?"

Ben placed a sleeve of macaroni and cheese boxes on a low shelf, then stood upright, clicking his pricing gun in time to the song that played over the store's speaker system. "Nope. She had family business today and left me in charge. Need something?"

"Just to say hi to my friend. *Hi.*"

They chatted for a few minutes and then Jennifer let him get back to work. A half an hour and a full cartload of groceries later, she was ready to head home and lay out her lesson plan once and for all.

Only, her car had other ideas.

She screamed as a giant *tha-thump* sounded beneath her, and she pulled over to the side of the road in utter panic.

"Oh, please. Oh, please, don't let it be a dog or cat or bunny or turtle or . . . Oh, *please*, let it be a stick or a rock or a cardboard box," she prayed, rushing out of the car and searching for whatever it was she'd just hit. No squished fluff or broken shell lay anywhere in sight. Instead, an angry, rusted heap of metal sat several yards back.

"What the—Did that come from *you?*" she asked her car who, of course, did not respond.

Seeing as no other cars were in sight, she raced back up the road and grabbed the junky engine part, then raced back and threw it on the floor of her passenger seat. "I'll figure out what to do with you later," she said to the hunk of metal spitting grease stains all over her floor mats.

With a quick twist of the key, she was ready to get back on the road. But the car was less ready. In fact, its engine wouldn't turn over or make any sound at all.

"Ugh!" she cried, pumping the brake and gas pedals, both to no avail.

She grabbed her dumb phone, which thankfully still had a full charge, and dialed up Elise. If her friend truly wanted to forever be saving someone, well, this was the perfect chance to help Jennifer out of a tight spot. Besides, her pickup truck could tow Jennifer and her wounded car over to the automotive shop, which seemed to be the only solution either of them had at the moment. Thankfully, she didn't have to wait much more than five minutes for her friend to show up at her side.

"I don't know what I'm going to do! I don't have

the money to fix it, and I'm supposed to pick up Molly Sue from school at two thirty. It's her first day. I can't be late, but how am I supposed to get there and how am I supposed to get her home? On piggy-back?" she cried, pacing the length of her car back and forth and back again.

"Jennifer, calm down already," Elise demanded while looping a cable around the car's lifted hood. "You don't know how much it's going to cost yet, and I'll pick up the kid. It's going to be fine. Now get in there and put yourself in neutral so I can tow you over to the auto shop."

Tom Hanson, owner of Sweet Grove Automotive, offered a bleaker assessment of the situation. "Why didn't you bring it in sooner? You could have fried your whole engine. As it is, the transmission is a mighty expensive part to replace."

Jennifer gasped, too shocked to speak.

Tom rushed forward with the options, ending with, "I could order a salvaged part to save you some money here. That'll only be a few hundred to replace and fix up."

"Three hundred! I don't have that kind of money!"

"It's better than a couple thousand. Or having to buy a whole new car, which could have very well been the alternative here. And you're not hurt. That's kind of a small miracle, too." He smiled up at her beneath shaggy blond hair, but when he caught sight of Jennifer's face, his expression immediately dampened.

"Look, I'll have to order in the part, and I'll do that now so you aren't left waiting without a car for too long. It'll be at least four days until I have what I need to get you on the road again, so that gives you time to come up with the money. I promise it'll be good as . . . well, it's never going to be good as new. This car's old enough to have its own driver's permit, for crying out loud. But we'll get 'er fixed. Don't you worry about that."

Jennifer forced back tears. God was bigger than her problems. She just needed to have faith and patience and all the other virtues that were especially hard to find when the going got tough. "Thank you, Tom. I really appreciate your help. I'll find the money and get it to you tomorrow if I can. Will you excuse me please?"

Seemed she didn't have much of a choice now. As much as she preferred to be more of a casual observer of her perfect sister's perfect life, she would need to reach out to Jessica for help. It was simply the only option she had at the moment.

Unfortunately, Jessica wasn't home.

Of course she wasn't. The middle of the day on a Monday? She was probably in court, earning her big lawyer bucks and making their parents proud in a way Jennifer never could.

She'd try again tonight after her time with Molly Sue. Maybe seeing Liam again would help lift her spirits, help remind her who she actually was. She hated the person she became whenever she needed to turn to her sister for help. For one thing, green had never been her color—especially when that green came with a heaping dose of envy.

She needed to slow down, count her blessings, and instead of fearing her sister, she needed to put a bit of faith in the Father.

ELEVEN

That Monday was a hard one for Liam. After driving into town and walking Molly Sue to her new classroom, he returned to his big, empty house all alone. Even though he spent so many of his waking hours locked in his office, this felt different, as if by knowing his happy, sweet daughter was just a hallway away had given him something extra every day before.

His life hadn't always been like this, for as much as he avoided change, change had always found him when he least wanted it. From a geeky kid to the star of the football team, all the way to a young Internet entrepreneur, to falling in love with an amazing woman and living a perfect life, to this new dark epoch—the world just couldn't make up its mind about what it wanted from Liam James.

Without his daughter around to brighten his day, would he fall into a new, darker era? Or would he ever manage to find happy days again? That seemed unlikely.

He thought of Jennifer and the meal they'd shared at Mabel's the day before. Even though he was by himself now, he wasn't alone anymore. She had reintroduced him to the town, affirmed that, yes, he was welcome here.

He should have warned Jennifer that Molly would do her level best to guilt her into giving her cookies as an after school snack. It had been something of a tradition when Molly had homeschooled with her mother. They'd finish up their lessons and then toast to another successful day of learning with Oreos and milk.

Megan had been far stricter and put an end to the cookie tradition, but every once in a while Liam would let Molly Sue sneak a few after her tutor had left. That made him wonder, why did he leave it to others to raise his child, to make sure she did her schoolwork or ate healthy meals? She needed extra help, so why hadn't he reduced his work hours in favor of being there for his little girl?

He liked being able to offer Jennifer work, and he liked having an excuse to see her on most days of the week, but he didn't like that he'd turned away from his daughter in her time of need. Maybe he could fix that, fix everything—or at least everything that was in his power to fix.

He could hire an assistant to help with the work load, take off full weekends, maybe take a vacation while he was at it. When it came right down to it, the most important thing in his life wasn't his company. It was Molly Sue. And he was forever entrusting her to others, so why couldn't he hire someone to help with work? Why couldn't he shift his priorities just enough to focus more on the little girl who needed the one parent she still had left?

Before he could talk himself out of it, he browsed to the school website and noted the dates for Spring Break. He still had a couple of months left to plan, to figure everything out. In two months, he could hire and train an assistant, Molly Sue could catch up and integrate into school, and he could plan the perfect family vacation. It would help the two of them reconnect, help them figure out how they related to each other when it was just the two of them, help them move forward in life together rather than simply side by side.

It would only take a little bit of planning, a little bit of change. So then why was it so terrifying?

* * *

Molly Sue and Rebecca
Thirteen months ago

Molly Sue closed her eyes as she breathed in the yummy smell of the gingerbread cookies left over from Christmas. They weren't as yummy as Oreos, but they were still really, really good. All of Christmas had been a blast. Mommy had surprised her with all kinds of wonderful gifts, including the blue necklace Molly loved so much. Daddy said it would be their last holiday all together, but Molly Sue didn't believe that. She prayed to God every single night before bed and asked if He could pretty please change His mind about taking her mommy to live with Him in Heaven.

She still did some schoolwork with her mommy at home. Now she studied with her new tutor, Megan, too, but Megan wasn't here for Christmas, so that left just Molly Sue and her mommy during the days—the way she liked best.

"You are doing such a great job with your reading, sweetie. I'm proud of you," Mommy said as she sat up crooked in the special bed the hospital had delivered so she could sleep in the living room and not worry about having to go up and down the stairs.

"Thank you, Mommy. I am working very hard like you asked me to." She brought her notebook closer to show her fresh page full of all the big cursive letters she'd learned.

Her mother smiled and then coughed. She coughed so much, Molly Sue thought she might never stop. But then finally she did and lay back against the bed. Mommy's skin looked gray and her face looked sad. "It won't be long now," she said after blowing out a big breath through her nose.

"Until you go to Heaven?"

She smiled, but Molly Sue saw a tear shiver in her mommy's eye.

"Maybe you don't have to go. I have been asking God very nicely if you can stay. I always remember to say please and everything."

"Molly Sue, it's not that easy." She coughed again, but it was only a little cough this time. "I'm very tired and have been resting up to save my energy for the big journey. I'm happy even though I will miss you and Daddy very much. God and my family who live in Heaven will all be waiting for me, and we're going to have a big party when I get there. Doesn't that sound fun?"

Molly Sue shrugged. Was a party really all that fun if you had to say goodbye to everyone you loved in order to get an invite?

"I've finished writing my letters to you. Do you remember that I was working on those?"

Molly nodded and smoothed out the wrinkles in her mother's blanket.

"I was going to wait to give them to you after Christmas, but I don't know how much longer I have."

Oh no. She was forgetting things again, and easy things, too. They had spent the whole day celebrating around the tree. Would she be able to remember Molly Sue once she left for Heaven, or would she lose all her Earth memories and have to start over like a baby? Molly Sue shivered. "Mommy, Christmas was two days ago. Remember?"

"Oh, that's right. Of course." Her mother shook her head and sighed. She closed her eyes and didn't open them again for a while. Molly Sue thought maybe she had fallen asleep, but when she turned to leave, her mother spoke out again.

"Molly Sue, have you been working on your writing?"

She looked down at the notebook she had shared only minutes before. Why was Mommy acting like she couldn't remember anything? Sometimes she was perfectly herself, and other times she looked at Molly Sue like maybe she didn't even know who her own daughter was.

"Mommy, I just showed you." She tried to be patient, but she was starting to feel scared again. She wanted God to leave her mommy here on Earth, but she wanted *her* mommy—not this woman who was quickly becoming a stranger.

"Oh? I'm sorry. I'm very tired. I know I don't always make sense anymore, but I wrote you letters. Have I given them to you yet?"

Molly Sue shook her head. She didn't like it when Mommy acted this way. Before it only happened sometimes, but now her mother seemed to be confused almost the whole day. Actually, it made Molly Sue wonder if a part of her had already left for Heaven without taking the rest.

"I need to give you the letters. They're very important. Let me just . . ." Her mother reached for the railings at the sides of her bed and tried to push herself up. She grunted and strained, but she didn't budge from that bed.

Molly Sue tried very hard not to cry, but she was getting scareder and scareder by the minute. What if Mommy died right now when Daddy was shut away in his office? What would she do, and would it be all her fault if Mommy died while trying to get the letters for Molly Sue?

"It won't be long now," Mommy said again. "I'm very tired all the time."

"I know, Mommy. You said that. You said you had letters for me, too. Maybe you can tell me where they are so I can go find them while you take a nap?"

"The letters are very important. They are about how you can be Daddy's angel, but they are only for you. Okay?"

"Mommy!" she shouted. She hated to yell, but she needed to find some way to get through, especially if the letters were every bit as important as her mother kept insisting. "Where are the letters? I will go find them now."

"I put them . . ." She paused and closed her eyes while she thought. "In the bottom of my big jewelry box, I think. Can you go get them and hide them some place where you'll remember but Daddy won't be able to find them?"

"Yes, I can put them inside my Elsa castle. Daddy never wants to play with that, so he won't find them there."

"That's perfect. You are so smart. That's why I knew I could trust you with this very important job." Mommy coughed and her knees fidgeted under the thin blanket draped over her on the bed.

Molly Sue took one more look back, and as she ran up the stairs to find the letters, she heard her mother say, "It won't be long now, Molly Sue. God is calling me home to Heaven."

* * *

With Elise's help, Jennifer was able to get her groceries home and unpacked. They even managed to pick up Molly Sue on time for her first lesson, too.

"Hi, Miss Elise!" Molly Sue said, wrapping her new friend in a hug. "Are you going to help me learn, too?"

Elise blew a raspberry. "Help you? Nah, I need to learn myself. I always liked gym class when I was your age. I need to learn science just as much as you do. Would it be okay if I stayed for the lesson, too?"

Molly swung her feet back and forth as she sat between Jennifer and Elise in the truck cab. "Yes, that'll be fun!"

Jennifer rolled her eyes but laughed all the same. "*Elise? Fun?* Nah, never."

"Quiet, you," Elise replied. "Don't make me turn this truck around."

They all giggled and continued to tell jokes for the rest of the short drive back to the apartment.

"Let's start with a quick snack," Jennifer said, searching in the fridge for the veggies she had chopped in the short period of time she'd managed to salvage between the auto shop and the drive to the elementary school.

Molly crinkled her nose. "I don't like cucumbers. Do you have any Oreos?"

So much for a healthy snack . . . "I guess that would be okay to celebrate our first day together, but tomorrow we're having something that's actually good for you. Got it?"

"Got it!"

She poured them all tall glasses of milk and placed a sleeve of cookies on the table. "You can have one now, and one after you finish your lesson."

Elise grabbed a couple of Oreos from the package.

"Same goes for you, too, missy!"

"She's strict," Elise whispered to Molly Sue, making sure it was loud enough so that Jennifer could hear.

Jennifer rolled her eyes and kind of wished she had a ruler she could slap on the table to bring their lesson to order. "It'll go by fast," she said, taking a seat beside Molly. "Learning always does when you make it fun, and I have a really cool project planned for today. I was looking on Pinterest last night and found all kinds of DIY science labs that are perfect for second graders like you, Molly Sue." She hooked an eyebrow at Elise. "And second grade-*like* students such as Elise."

They all burst into giggles again. Elise had never minded being ribbed as long as it was all in good fun.

"We're going to learn about how clouds make rain," Jennifer explained once they had all sobered up a bit. "It'll be a little messy, but *a lot* of fun. Maybe so fun you won't realize you're learning something new."

"I like you, Miss Elliott," the little girl said as Jennifer brought out clear plastic cups and shaving cream to prepare for their at-home experiment.

"I like you, too," she said, tousling Molly's curls. Moments like this were the very reason she'd become a teacher.

"And I like clouds, because Heaven is made of clouds. My mommy lives in Heaven, you know."

"Yes, I know." *Poor kid. She misses her mom so much.*

Molly Sue continued to sip her milk and speak in a matter of fact way. "My daddy misses her a lot."

"I bet he does. It's hard when you have to be apart from someone you love."

"Yeah, that's why he needs someone new to love." She winked at Elise, then giggled.

Jennifer knew her face had to be red as a lobster in the pot. Here she was ready to bust out the tissues and administer an emergency therapy lesson, but Molly Sue had totally flipped the script on her instead. She looked away and mumbled, "Um, I think that's probably a decision your daddy should make for himself."

Elise turned to Molly Sue. "Do you think your dad likes anybody specific?"

Molly Sue nodded between licks of her Oreo. "Yup, he likes Miss Elliott."

Well, at least she couldn't get any redder than she already was. And why would Molly Sue say that Liam liked her unless it was actually true? He didn't seem like the type to gush about his feelings to anyone, let alone his seven-year-old child. Still, Jennifer felt her heart speed up. She even got a little light-headed and had to sink into the chair for support.

It didn't matter that Jennifer had no idea how to respond, because Elise had an answer for everything. "Oooh!" she cooed. "Somebody's got a crush!"

"Yup!" Molly Sue laughed, then patted Jennifer's arm to get her attention. "Do you like my daddy, too?" she asked with huge, innocent eyes.

Jennifer took a deep breath and forced herself to answer. "He's, uh, a very nice man and a good friend." *How about a topic change, please!* "Your mom was my friend, too, you know."

Molly Sue refused to take the bait. "But do you *like* like him?"

"Molly," Jennifer warned, placing her hands in her lap so that neither of the others would see how they shook. "Are we here to talk about boys, or are we here to learn science?"

"Science," Molly Sue mumbled.

"Science," Elise mumbled.

"Good," Jennifer said. "Moving on . . ."

TWELVE

Liam pressed the buzzer for Jennifer's apartment, remembering in vivid detail the last time he had pushed that button and the half-naked woman he'd found on the other side of that door. He shook his head to reorient himself, then jogged up the stairs to say hello.

"Hi, Liam." Jennifer appeared a bit scattered as she welcomed him inside. "Hey, Elise, can you take Molly Sue to play outside while I talk to her dad?"

"Sure thing, teach. C'mon, kiddo." Elise stopped at the open door and waited for Molly to pass through before her.

"How did today go?" he asked once the door had latched behind them.

"Come sit with me at the table. I have some—actually, *all*—of the veggies left over from our after-school snack. Let me go grab them."

Liam chuckled when Jennifer set a neatly arranged circle of sliced cucumbers with a tub of dip set in the middle. "Let me guess. She guilted you into giving her Oreos?"

"How did you know?" she asked around the cucumber she had just popped into her mouth.

"I know my child, and that is classic Molly Sue, especially when cucumbers are involved." He laughed, but Jennifer did not join in.

"Well, did you know she's trying to set you up?" she blurted out before sinking into the chair opposite him at the table.

"Now *that* I did not know. Who is she trying to set me up with?" He knew the answer before he asked, but he wanted her to confirm it for him.

"Um, me." Jennifer turned beet red—no, redder than that, maybe as red as a cooked lobster.

"This is *new information*," he mumbled. "I'm sorry if she put you on the spot, especially in front of your friend."

Jennifer glanced out the window and smirked. "Elise? Please. She is probably just as much to blame as Molly Sue. I mean, who knows what they were chattering away about at lunch yesterday?" She was embarrassed, that much was obvious. But was she embarrassed because Molly Sue had hit the nail on the head with her matchmaking endeavors? Unfortunately, it was hard for Liam to tell. Perhaps if he kept the conversation going, he'd know soon whether she returned his interest in her. More than likely, this was all a big mistake on everyone's part. She could reject him kindly, and he could move past all this with zero guilt.

Liam rose and went to stand by the window, watching Molly Sue and Elise play a game of hopscotch in the parking lot. "No, I think she did this on her own," he admitted. "That explains all the winking she's been doing this past week. It explains a lot, actually."

Jennifer remained seated at the table, and he turned back toward her, taking in the slight tremor of her hands and the mixed energy that hung in the air. *She could be feeling anything. Why are women so hard to read?* "I'm sorry she dragged you into this."

"Don't be." She smiled, her hands steadying as she did.

Meanwhile, Liam's breath hitched, taking the words clear out of his mouth. Was this the moment? Would he and Jennifer—

Before he could finish his thought, she continued.

"I'm very flattered, but I know it's all just a little girl's imagination run wild. You're still grieving Rebecca. As you should be." She continued to smile as if doing so would soften the rejection, but was it a rejection at all? This was so confusing, and Molly Sue's blatant matchmaking hadn't done a lick of good.

"Yes, yes, that's right." And it was true—he still missed Rebecca every day, but he also now thought of Jennifer every day. How much could change in such a short period of time, the story of his life.

She cleared her throat and raised a hand to the back of her neck. "Anyway, let me catch you up on what we learned today. Molly is exceptionally bright, and . . ."

He took in the words as Jennifer recounted the lesson plan from that afternoon along with her plans for the rest of the week. What he couldn't take in was any true understanding of how the woman beside him felt. Had she wanted him to admit to the crush? Had she expected him to make some kind of declaration? To grab her in a soul-shaking kiss?

And by not doing any of that, had he just blown whatever little chance he had?

* * *

Jennifer said goodbye to her visitors all at once, then watched as Liam's sedan and Elise's truck pulled away from her apartment building, one after the other. What a strange day it had been, from the car breaking down to the unexpected prodding by Molly Sue, and especially the awkward conversation with Liam that followed. If she'd read him right, it seemed he actually did have feelings for her and may have even wanted to ask her on a date.

That is, before she stupidly told him it was too soon. Best case, he would take his time and try asking her out again after a few months or years. Worst case, he would assume she wasn't interested and eventually move on—with someone else.

Part of her wished she could turn back the clock and play her role in that scene differently, but another hummed with relief. He was cute and kind and made her feel a bit like floating through the air. But *so what?*

There had been attractive men in her world before, and there would be attractive men again someday, when she was actually ready to return their affections. Right now, she needed to focus on ironing out the wrinkles in her financial situation. Besides, if she clung to Liam now, wouldn't he think she wanted him for his money? Did part of her want him for that reason? Life would certainly be easier were she not living on the edge of poverty.

But no, she liked Liam for many reasons, and his luxury lifestyle was not one of them. It didn't seem to make him happy, and she doubted it would make her happy either. No, she loved his courage, sensitivity, and authenticity. That's what she liked about Liam James.

Still, they came from two entirely different worlds. He was filet mignon, and she was ground chuck. And even though she'd spoken out of turn, she'd been *right*. He still clearly grieved the loss of Rebecca, and for that matter, so did she.

Her phone rang through the open window, and she took the stairs two at a time to grab it before the caller could hang up.

"Hello?" she asked breathless, then shivered from the chill. Why had she opened her window at this time of night? At this time of year?

"Sorry I missed your call earlier," her sister Jessica said, skipping the formality of saying hello herself. "You sounded pretty upset. What's going on?"

Jennifer had already told her everything—or at least everything about the car and rent and job—in her voicemail, but leave it to her lawyer sister to make sure she had all the facts before making any move toward solving the problem.

Jennifer slunk down onto her couch and hugged her Pusheen throw pillow to her chest, then transitioned Jessica to speaker. "My hours got cut down at work, and my car died. I don't have enough money to make rent, let alone pay out of pocket to fix my stupid car."

Jessica didn't miss a beat. "Your hours got cut down. Did you lose your benefits?"

"Yes." Jennifer sighed.

"Then you're lucky it's only your car that's in trouble. What if something happened to you healthwise?"

"I don't know," Jennifer mumbled as she picked lint off her pillow and frowned. "I'm trying my best, but this is the hand I was dealt."

"Well, I'll send you the money for repairs, obviously. Sign up for healthcare dot gov and have them forward the bills to me. And how much do you need for rent?"

"Jessica, stop. I appreciate that you want to help, but just enough for the car will be fine."

"I don't think so. What if you get into an accident, break a bone? What if you get cancer? You'd be screwed without health insurance."

Cancer—the same ugly disease that had taken Rebecca, and her sister knew that, too. Was she trying to kick Jennifer when she was down or what? She swallowed back that particular reminder. It was bad enough she had to beg for help. She didn't need a fight on top of that.

"I'll figure something out, Jess. I swear."

"You know, with as little as you make, you could probably get Medicaid. Have you looked into that?"

"No, I—"

"Why don't you come to Baltimore and stay with us for a while? I bet you could find a new job in a heartbeat."

Dear God, please don't let it come to that.

"I'm happy in Sweet Grove, Jess. Please understand, I don't like having to ask for help, and I wouldn't if I had any other option. Can you maybe deactivate super lawyer mode and just be my sister right now?"

Jessica groaned. "It would be easier to be your sister if you called me more just to chat and less because you needed rescuing."

It hurt, but her sister did have a point. Jennifer had always been the damsel in distress, and Jessica had always been the princess in shining silks, swooping in to rescue her. Most of the time, Jennifer didn't actually need help, but her sister showed her love by fixing things. Actions were easier than words. She thought about pointing that out, but instead said, "You're right. I'm sorry. It's just hard sometimes, you know?"

Jessica's voice softened. "What's hard?"

At the moment, many things were hard, but Jennifer chose to focus on the difficulties that pertained to her family instead of all the other stuff. "Like the more we talk about our lives, the more I realize you aren't here anymore. I miss you. I miss Mom and Dad. I miss the girls. I check in on Facebook every day, sometimes more than once. I like seeing what you're up to, even though I'm not there with you. Kelsie and Jamie are getting so big! I feel like I'm missing out on their whole lives."

"You kind of are, Jenn. Missing it, I mean. We all miss you, too. You don't want to move to the city; that's fine, but at least come for a visit. Hey, actually . . ." Her sister's voice grew distant, and Jennifer wondered if the line had died or if maybe she'd been hung up on.

"Jess?" she shouted.

"Sorry, I'm back. I was just searching through my calendar to grab the dates. We're planning a trip to Disneyland for spring break. It'll be a surprise for the girls. You should come with us. Want to?"

She did want to. That sounded like lots of fun, but she knew Jess would have to pay her way on top of helping her out of the current car predicament. Would it be worth it? She hated accepting charity from her friends, so why did she allow it from her family?

"I'll think about it."

"You'll do it. Fourth week of March. Pack warm. We can layover in Austin and catch you there. Sound like a plan?"

"Jess, I'll think about it."

"See you soon, sis."

THIRTEEN

Liam felt a kick on the back of his seat. Molly's whine followed shortly after. "I'm hungry, Daddy!"

"We'll be home in about half an hour." He glanced at his daughter in the rearview mirror, but she had her eyes focused outside the window and her arms crossed heavily across her chest. Uh-oh, they were on the verge of a meltdown. "What do you want me to make for dinner tonight?"

"No, I'm hungry now!" she screamed and kicked him again.

"And you can't wait?" he asked, catching her eye in the rearview mirror.

She shook her head adamantly and pouted. "No. I need to eat *now*, or I will starve to death."

"Fine, fine." He redirected the car toward Ernie's, shutting out his daughter's complaints as he drove. Luckily, it wasn't even five minutes before they'd made it to the restaurant and taken their seats at a small table in the corner. The old man Ernie himself came to take their orders.

"Can we start with some soup, please?" Liam pointed to Molly Sue. "She's starving."

Molly Sue nodded, and a moment later, they each had piping hot bowls of soup and a basket of bread to go with it.

"So . . ." he began while Molly Sue slurped hungrily on her soup.

She looked up at him but didn't make any signs of slowing down.

"Did you have a good first day of school?"

She gave him the thumbs-up with her free hand. *Well, at least she's not a crank anymore.*

"Did you make any new friends?"

She kept her thumb held high as she continued to eat.

"I'm sorry I've been so busy with work lately," he offered. Maybe now was a good time to have a heart-to-heart. It would be easier if she just listened. Otherwise, he might lose the nerve. "I just signed a new retainer with a large franchise owner before coming to pick you up today. But you don't care about any of that, do you?"

"That's not true," she mumbled, keeping her mouth closed as she spoke so the soup wouldn't spill out.

Not the response he'd expected. He had no idea what she meant by this casual accusation. "What's not true?"

She swallowed with one big gulp and set her spoon down in the now empty bowl. "The reason you work so much. It's because you're sad and miss Mommy."

Molly Sue leaned forward in her chair and reached her hand toward his. When he took it, she rubbed her fingers over his palm and said, "It's okay, Daddy. I miss her, too."

"How did you—"

"Mommy told me." She let go of his hand and picked up a warm piece of bread. "She explained that you worked extra so you won't remember how much you miss her."

"Well, that's true, and I'll never stop missing your mom, but I *am* going to stop working so much. I'm going to take some more time off so that we can do more things together. Would you like that?"

Molly Sue smiled as she bit into her bread. "*Mmm hmm.*"

"Good. I was thinking we could take a vacation, and—"

"You should invite Miss Elliott, too."

"Miss Elliott?"

"Yup."

"On vacation?"

"Yup, and to dinner, and to our house, and on a date."

He frowned. "She told me about your little matchmaking efforts tonight."

"You're welcome," she said around a full mouth of mushed bread. Suddenly, he'd lost his appetite.

"What? No. You shouldn't have done that."

Molly seemed unaware of how uncomfortable she had made everything about this evening. "Done what? Told her you like her?"

"But I—"

"But you do, and she likes you, too."

He sighed and pressed his fingers to his temples to stave off an oncoming stress headache. "Now you listen to me, Molly Sue. This is all grown-up business. It's not up to you to set me up on dates. When I'm ready to go out with a woman, I will ask her myself."

"No, you won't. That's a lie, Daddy. I know you like Miss Elliott, and I think she likes you, too. And it *is* my business. It's my job."

"What's your job? I don't remember hiring you to run my love life."

Molly Sue rolled her eyes and spoke slowly as if it were the only way to make him understand something obvious to her. "It is my job, Daddy. I'm your angel."

Her job? My angel?

None of this made sense to him. Why was she clinging so tightly to the idea of setting him up with Jennifer Elliott when she couldn't even keep her favorite color or her favorite Disney princess straight for more than a few days at a time?

Had he been working so hard for so long that his own daughter had become a stranger?

The next day, a check from Jennifer's sister arrived via Next Day Air. It was for triple the amount Jennifer had requested, and so she vowed to pay Jessica back the first moment she had even an extra dime to give.

When she paid at the shop, Tom Hanson gave her a loaner car, which meant she could avoid any more of Elise goading Molly Sue on during their after-school lessons. Whether from the absence of Elise or something else altogether, the silly talk of matching her with Liam had died down.

Was it simply because Jennifer did an excellent job keeping Molly Sue focused on her studies? Or had Liam had a heart-to-heart with his daughter and told her to knock it off?

The days passed one at a time, the same as they always had. Jennifer and Liam exchanged polite words whenever he came to pick up Molly Sue from her lessons, but Jennifer also felt as if he had made a conscious decision to shut her out somewhere along the way.

She'd embarrassed him. She'd pushed him too hard or, worse still, she'd rejected him, hurt him. Neither alternative appealed to her in the least, but what could she do?

Nothing, that was what.

She'd thought she'd moved on, but she'd been a fool. Seeing him that night had lit something in her, made the longing that much more intense. Feelings of love didn't just go away, no matter how much she might like them to.

Oh, why did she have to fall for Liam, of all people? He'd never stop carrying a torch for Rebecca, which meant he'd never be available. It didn't matter how much her heart fluttered when she caught sight of him, didn't matter how much she thought they could be happy together, complete each other in a way they both needed.

Love happened—well, in her case, love didn't happen. But that was fine, just fine. One day she'd like somebody new, and until then, she was doing good by helping a little girl who needed it. Soon Molly Sue would be all caught up with her lessons, and Jennifer would have enough to pay back her sister. Everything would go back to normal. She'd still need another job to make ends meet, but ranch season would be upon them then. She could work extra hard during that time to make sure she was set for the year.

Everything would be fine—better than fine. So why did she have such a hard time believing that?

She'd been perfectly happy in her simple, small life, until God had tempted her with the possibility of more. If this was a test, did it mean she had failed? And why would God even want to test her? She'd always done His will, spread His love. It didn't seem fair that He would torment her like this.

Jennifer thought of Job, who had endured far greater tests at the hands of their Lord. She shuddered as she pictured her body peppered with boils. God had taken everything and everyone from Job. Jennifer had hardly suffered at all, not really. She needed to stop being so dramatic.

"God, I'm not happy with you," she said aloud. "It's one thing to test me, but Liam could get seriously hurt. He's already been hurt. Haven't you given him enough of a cross to bear?"

She thumbed through her Bible and reread the story of Job, then let out a huge sigh.

"I know I'm not the first person to ever feel like you're testing them, and I won't be the last. You know I'm a faithful servant, but could you just go ahead and reveal thy will already?

"I'm going to read this, and I'm going to do whatever it says. So please be obvious. Could you? Please?" She flipped through the pages of her Bible, landing on a page at random as she often liked to do when looking for guidance. Of course, God wasn't a Magic 8-Ball, but sometimes viewing His words in the context of her dilemmas gave her a new understanding. Other times, it raised more questions than it answered.

She glanced down at the page and immediately recognized the section. "First John four, eh?" She looked up toward the ceiling for a moment, then back down at her Bible.

And she read.

Beloved, do not believe every spirit, but test the spirits, whether they are of God; because many false prophets have gone out into the world.

"Yes, I know that," she answered. "Are these feelings a test? Are they false?" She kept reading until she reached the next paragraph.

Beloved, let us love one another, for love is of God, and everyone who loves is born of God and knows God. He who does not love does not know God, because God is love.

"Okay, I think I know where this is going." She smiled to herself and read on, ending when she reached:

God abides in us, and His love is perfected in us.

"Amen," she whispered. She contemplated these words in her heart before speaking again. "So this isn't a test? It's a gift?"

God did not speak back but had already given the answer in her heart.

"Thank you for your blessing, but I think I need to get one from somebody else first, too. Please give me the right words."

She grabbed a light jacket and headed out to take a drive. She hoped her old friend would understand what she needed to request of her.

FOURTEEN

Liam only had a few minutes with Molly Sue that evening. He picked her up from Jennifer's apartment, then turned right back around to take her to her friend Josie's house for a sleepover. He'd hoped that by remaining focused on business, his silly crush would fade. But when his hand had brushed against Jennifer's when they both reached for Molly's forgotten notebook, an intense spark flew through his veins and into his heart.

Why did he have to fall for Jennifer Elliott, of all people? She had been his wife's close friend, and the two women were so very similar besides. Did he actually like Jennifer for Jennifer, or was it just that she reminded him of what he'd lost?

Maybe he was just grateful to her for being the

first person to welcome him and Molly Sue back to Sweet Grove. There were countless reasons he liked her, but none of them explained his growing desire to take her in his arms and never let go.

And he hadn't been thinking about Rebecca when they'd been together at the restaurant, sharing town gossip and flirting with each other. That was all Jennifer.

Only Jennifer.

He resisted the urge to drive back to her apartment after he dropped Molly Sue off at her friend's. Just because he liked her didn't mean she returned those feelings. He felt like he was back in school himself. Only school had been far easier when it came to women. He'd been the star football player and only had to mumble a quick "hi" for girls to throw their numbers at him. Things became more complex as an adult, especially as an adult with a child. His interest could no longer be casual. The possibility of marriage was implied by his very interest.

Talk about pressure!

At home, he trudged inside and dropped Molly Sue's school bag onto the entryway floor. A sad beeping noise sounded from inside. *What now?* he wondered, turning back to collect the bag.

After clearing out all of Molly's folders, books, and binders from inside, he found one of Molly's

Disney critters nestled at the bottom of the bag. He also found her mother's delicate sapphire pendant. He'd need to have a talk with her about what was and wasn't okay to take to school.

For now, he'd just log a few hours of client work and then hit the hay early. He carefully packed Molly Sue's school supplies back into her bag, but when he lifted a small notebook, a yellowed paper fluttered to the ground. It had been folded over several times and the ink had faded near the creases.

Did Molly Sue have a crush of her own? Was this a second-grade love note? If so, she must have read it hundreds of times over in the span of just a few short weeks since she'd begun at Sweet Grove Elementary.

He wanted to respect her privacy, but more than that, he needed to protect his daughter. Telling himself he was doing the right thing, he unfolded the note, prepared to laugh at a cute conversation between friends. He was not prepared for what he found in its place.

Rebecca's careful handwriting filled the page. Tears tugged at his eyes, and he quickly wiped them away so he could read.

———

My dearest daughter,

This is my first letter to you, but I promise there will be just as many more as I am able to write. If you're reading this now, then I have probably already left for Heaven. I love and miss you very much! And of course, I can miss you all the way from Heaven. Don't argue with your mother!

Liam laughed. Rebecca had always possessed a spunky sense of humor. It was one of the many things he loved about her.

Enough joking, though, because I have something very serious to talk about with you. Remember that time Pastor Bernie's dog, Bruno, escaped and was missing for days before one day he showed up in our yard? You saw him through the window and ran to bring him inside before he could wander off again. We drove him back to Pastor Bernie that day, and he said he'd been praying very hard but had almost lost faith Bruno would ever come home. He said you were an angel of the Lord sent to help him and his dog find each other again, then he gave us cookies and lemonade to celebrate and even thanked you by name in the big church the following Sunday, too! That was a great day, right?

Well, now I need you to put your wings and halo back on, because it's time to be an angel again—an angel for a very important person we both love lots.

Daddy.

I'll tell you more next time I write, but for now just know that I love you, that I've always loved you, and I always will.

Hugs and kisses all the way from Heaven, Your mommy

Liam sniffed and folded the paper carefully, just the way Molly Sue had left it. What did Rebecca mean that Molly Sue needed to be an angel for him? And where were the other letters? He tore through the backpack again, carefully searching each pocket, each book, each small zippered area, but he couldn't find any other notes.

Did Rebecca ever have the chance to write more? He was glad she'd left behind pieces of herself for their daughter, but knowing she hadn't done the same for him made him feel so very far away.

He needed to see her, needed to talk to her, needed to find out more.

And so he placed the folded note in his shirt pocket, pulled the car from the garage, and headed toward the cemetery where he'd laid her to rest.

* * *

Molly Sue and Rebecca
Twelve months ago

Molly Sue sat on the edge of her mommy's bed. The sun shone bright outside, even though the room inside was dark and dim.

"Molly?" her mother called.

"I'm right here." She gripped her hand, hating how cold it felt inside her own.

"Is Daddy here?" She stared out through drooping eyelids.

"He went to the store to get more groceries."

"That's for the best. I need to talk to you." She motioned for Molly Sue to come closer, but her daughter hesitated.

"About being Daddy's angel?"

"Yes. I think today is the day." She paused to let that sink in. "I'm leaving for Heaven, Molly Sue, so I have to tell you about the letters right now."

"You already gave me the letters. I have them in my Elsa castle." She'd already read them over many times, too. Molly Sue needed to make sure she understood, make sure that she was ready. And Molly thought she could do a good job being Daddy's angel, but she just wasn't ready to say goodbye to her mommy. Not now, not ever.

"Did you read them?" Her mother licked her cracked lips. She looked so different than the pretty, happy mommy Molly Sue knew. She'd gotten very skinny and weak. It frightened Molly to look at her. This was not how she wanted to remember her mommy, not one bit.

"I've read them lots of times," she confessed.

"I wrote you ten letters," Mommy went on. "I tried to keep the words simple, because they are so important. Did you understand what they said?"

"Yes, I think so." She hesitated again. "I just don't understand how I'll know it's time."

"You'll know. I promise, you'll know." Mommy tried to sit up but didn't make it very far. "What day is it today?"

"It's three weeks after Christmas. I don't know the exact day, though. Do you want me to call Daddy and ask?" she suggested. Daddy would know what to do, and if Mommy was right about leaving today, then he needed to be here with them.

"No, don't do that." Mommy let out a raspy chuckle. "Christmas, huh?"

"Yes, it was three weeks ago. You gave me your blue necklace. Remember?" She held up the pendant from around her neck, and it caught the light, creating a shiny shadow on the wall.

"Okay, then here's what you can do. Wait for one more Christmas to go by. Give Daddy time to miss me for a bit. It's okay to feel sad for a while. It's just not okay to stay sad forever. And the same goes for you, too, Miss Molly Sue."

"Okay, I'll try." Molly wasn't sure she could do what her mother was asking, though. She hadn't even left yet, and already Molly Sue felt so very sad like she could cry a whole ocean of tears.

"I know you will." Mommy closed her eyes and took in a big breath through her nose. "Will you help prop me up?"

Molly Sue lifted her mother against the big headboard and placed a pillow behind her back. It made her sad when she noticed how light and easy lifting Mommy had become. Little girls shouldn't have to pick up their mommies. That's supposed to be the mommy's job.

"Thank you," her mother said. "Now look at me while I talk to you, because I want to make sure we understand each other."

Molly Sue sat close to Mommy and held her hand.

"The letters, you said you read them. Tell me then, what are they about? I want to make sure you're ready to do your job. It's a big job, an important job, and I want to answer all your questions before I go."

"It's about being Daddy's angel."

"And how do you do that?"

She understood, but she didn't like it. "I have to find a new mommy to take your place."

"No," Mommy said with such force it startled poor Molly Sue. "Not to replace me. That's not it at all. The new mommy will be my helper. She'll take care of you and Daddy on Earth while I watch over you from Heaven."

"Like Santa's elves?"

Mommy smiled. "Yes, exactly like that."

There was still another very important thing Molly Sue didn't understand about the plan. "But who will the new Mommy be?"

Her mother closed her eyes as she talked. "I don't know yet, but you know who does? *God.* God knows, and He'll reveal His plan to us when He's ready. There are lots of nice ladies in town, and maybe some new ladies will move to town after I've gone. Anyone could be the perfect helper. You need to watch and wait, see who makes Daddy smile the biggest, see who makes you feel special and happy, too. Trust in God, and I know you'll find somebody wonderful to complete this family."

"I don't want a new mommy," Molly Sue sobbed. "I want you to stay. Please don't go, Mama."

Her mother reached up a shaky head to stroke Molly Sue's curls. "I don't want to go, but God needs me. We can't say no to God, can we? And remember about that huge welcome party I'll have once I get to Heaven? You know what the best part is, though? I won't hurt anymore, Molly Sue. I have hurt so very much these past few months, but the thing that hurts most of all is thinking about how much I'll miss you and Daddy and knowing how much you'll both miss me, too."

Molly Sue buried her face in Mommy's pajamas. She wanted to be brave and strong, but she was tired, too—tired of waiting for Mommy to go, of knowing that any minute could be the very last one she'd ever have with her.

"There, there." Mommy patted her back and allowed Molly to cry as much as she wanted, which as it turned out was a whole very lot.

"I have a present for you," she said after a while.

"More letters?" Molly Sue sniffed, and Mommy smiled.

"Kind of. They're letters I wrote in my diary when

I was younger about growing up in Sweet Grove and later falling in love with your daddy. I stopped writing when I became a mom. I was just so busy soaking in every minute I could with you. I wish I would've kept writing so you could know how much I loved you then, how much I love you now, and how much I will always love you every single day for the rest of your life."

Molly cried so hard, she could barely get the words out. "I love you, too, Mommy."

"It can be hard to hang on to memories as you get older. New memories come, and sometimes you don't have space for all of them. My hope is that by giving you my diaries, you will always know me. Even if you forget, you can read them and remember. I put them in the bottom drawer of my dresser. Can you go get them?"

Molly Sue reluctantly left her mother's embrace and tiptoed across the room, up the stairs, and to the dresser in her parents' room. Two stacks of three diaries each sat waiting for her amid several pairs of pants her mother hadn't worn since before she'd gotten sick. She carefully removed them from the drawer and brought them back down to Mommy.

"Open it," her mother said, resting her head back and looking up at the ceiling.

"It's the funny *S*," Molly Sue said with a sad smile as she trailed her finger over the old, faded ink.

"This is why I taught you cursive even though I could have written my letters to you in print. I wanted you to be able to start reading my diaries right away, to help get you through the sadness from when I first have to leave. The beginning will be the hardest, but it will get easier after that, I promise."

Molly Sue was afraid to ask, but she just had to know. "Mommy, are you leaving today?"

"I think so," she replied. "Come cuddle with me again."

Molly Sue set the journals on the side table and wrapped herself in her mother's arms for what felt like would be the last time ever. They continued to talk softly about the letters, the diaries, their favorite memories.

A while later, Daddy came home and sat with them, too. He did most of the talking from then on, brushing Mommy's hair from her eyes, kissing her eyelashes, and saying over and over again how much he loved her.

Molly Sue fell asleep there in her mommy's arms, and when she woke up again, Daddy explained that Mommy had fallen asleep, too, but that she wouldn't be waking up again.

She's with God and the angels now, Molly Sue told

herself, but it didn't stop her from feeling a deep, deep sadness.

Daddy asked her to go to her room for a few minutes so he could be alone with Mommy and then call the people who needed to come to take her body away. She stayed outside the door and listened as her father cried in pain. He said words, but Molly Sue couldn't tell what they were because he was crying so hard.

I should tell him about the letters now. I should start my job early, make him happy again.

She wanted so badly to make Daddy feel better, but she had made a promise to her mother, something she would never in her whole life be able to do again.

She needed to wait until the time was right. She needed to do this for her daddy, but even more so for her mommy.

And she would.

She would be the angel they both needed.

Before heading to the cemetery, Jennifer stopped at Morning Glories to buy a single yellow rose. Even though she couldn't afford a full bouquet, she knew her friend would appreciate the splash of bright, happy color amid all the bleak, depressing white flowers that regularly adorned the graveyard.

"You seem troubled," the florist, Iris, said as she rung Jennifer up at the register. "Want to talk about it?"

Jennifer shook her head. She hated to be rude, but she also needed to get to her friend as fast as possible. "I do need to talk about it, but specifically with Rebecca."

Iris nodded. "Ah, heading out to the Tender Hearts Memorial, then. Drive carefully. These old bones tell me a storm might be rolling in tonight."

Iris's parrot, Sunny Sunshine, made a happy clucking noise from his stand by the register, and the florist paused to scratch his head. Jennifer worked hard to be patient. She'd always admired how Iris lived her life one moment at a time rather than trying to plan too far ahead. Jennifer had always been like that, too, but now she had a hard time focusing on anything but the conversation ahead—one-sided or not, she knew it would give her the answers she so desperately needed.

Iris placed the little orange bird on her shoulder and returned to the register. "Sunny Sunshine feels the rain coming, too. He loves watching it roll down the window panes." She handed Jennifer her change and the rose.

"Thanks for the tip and for the flower." Jennifer waved goodbye, but Iris stopped her before she could go.

"Yes, these hip joints don't lie. Rain is on its way, and rain is exactly what I need for my garden to bloom. Did Summer tell you I planted a special garden for her and Ben's wedding this May? It won't be long now."

Patience is a virtue, Jennifer reminded herself again. *Iris is just being friendly.* "That's very nice, but . . ."

The florist pulled out the collar of her T-shirt, and her sun conure burrowed in and popped his head back out, making a happy quack noise as he closed his eyes. "Rain makes everything fresh. We need it to wash away the old and grow the new. Keep that in mind, won't you?"

"How did you . . . ?" Jennifer wasn't sure if she was more distracted by the two-headed florist or by her oddly relevant advice.

Iris laughed, and Sunny Sunshine mimicked her. "Honey, when you're as old as I am, you pick up a thing or two. Now go. Perhaps you can beat the storm."

Jennifer took a deep breath and headed back into the open air. A light misting drizzle had already begun to fall. But she couldn't turn back now. Even if it meant getting soaked as she visited her friend, this was just something she needed to do—and she needed to do now, before she lost this newfound conviction.

One way or the other, she had to decide what she wanted.

Any decision she came to wouldn't impact just the two of them, but also Molly Sue. A relationship with Liam meant opening her heart to his daughter, too. While she already cared for the little girl very much, taking on the role of mother was far different than simply being her tutor or Sunday school teacher.

Still, God's message had come through loud and clear as she'd read from her Bible that night. He hadn't put these feelings in her heart as a test. They were a gift. But would this gift benefit more than just her? That's what she needed to find out. She'd know when she saw Rebecca's headstone. She didn't know how or why, only that clarity would come.

A short while later, she pulled into Tender Hearts Memorial and found a parking spot on the twisted gravel road alongside the hill where Rebecca was laid to rest. Despite the death all around the cemetery, the grass glowed green with life. Iris was right about the rain making things grow. Rain made rainbows, too, a special promise from God.

Boom!

The first peal of thunder rumbled overhead, unleashing a mighty torrent in its wake. No, this wouldn't stop her. She still needed to see Rebecca. She couldn't let a little storm stop her. She only needed a moment with her friend, and then she would know.

Crash!

Lightning snaked through the sky, adding eerie illumination to the many graves planted in the memorial garden. It also brought to light a dark figure hunched over a grave—Rebecca's grave.

"Hey!" she called.

Liam turned to face her. His wet hair clung to his forehead, his shirt to his chest. He looked the very definition of bedraggled.

But when he saw her, *he smiled.*

FIFTEEN

One moment, Liam sat crying in the rain, begging either God or Rebecca to grant him an answer, give him a sign. And the next, he sat in the passenger seat of Jennifer's car as the two of them watched raindrops strike the windshield like tiny, angry missiles.

"What are you doing here?" he asked with a shiver, whether from the cold or the coincidence of finding her here, he didn't know. Perhaps it was a bit of both.

She fiddled with the air vents tucked into the dash, repositioning this way and that for maximum warmth. "What were *you* doing standing outside in the rain?" she shot back. "You'll catch your . . ."

"Death?" he asked morosely.

"It's just an expression. I didn't mean . . ." She frowned, but nothing could shake his own smile. He finally knew what he wanted. Now he just needed to figure out how to tell her.

"I know." He pointed at the yellow rose that lay forgotten on the dashboard. "Is that for Rebecca? Yellow always was her favorite, yet somehow I always end up bringing white when I come."

"I know," she answered, her smile returning. "Yellow is my favorite, too."

"You two are a lot alike."

She turned to study him, waiting to speak until his eyes journeyed over to meet hers. "Does that bother you?"

"At first it did," he admitted. "Having you around sometimes makes me miss her more, but sometimes it also makes me forget to feel sad."

She turned toward the windshield again, staring out at the wall of water. "What are you trying to say?" she whispered, almost as if she were afraid to voice the question any louder.

"It's like all the things I loved about her, I find in you, too. They're the same in a way, but different in another way. And all those things, I like that I'm finding them in you."

She folded her hands in her lap, and he could see

they were shaking. "Liam, do you like me in that way?" she asked without meeting his gaze.

"I didn't know my heart was still open, but yes, it seems you snuck inside." His smile grew when he caught the glimpse of understanding flash across her pretty face.

A small smiled played at her lips but quickly vanished. "Liam, please. I'm so confused. I need a straight answer to help me better understand." She still wouldn't look at him.

He turned in his seat and placed a gentle hand on her cheek, turning her to face him. He held his eyes steady on hers as he spoke, "I don't know why or how, only the way I feel. Yes, Jennifer, I like you very much. So much it terrifies me."

She placed her hand over his and sighed. "I know what you mean. All of it. I've been trying to explain away my feelings, but no matter how hard I try, I just can't. I asked God for a sign and He sent me here. To you."

He wanted to kiss her more than anything, but words were important now, and he needed his to be heard. "What if He's trying to push us together? Do you think God would do that?"

She pulled his hand from her cheek and held it in her lap, stroking his fingers with hers. "He's God," she said thoughtfully. "He totally does crazy things all the time, but He always has a reason."

"What do you suppose His reason is this time?" Another shiver swept through him, and he knew it wasn't the cold. A warmth started in his heart and moved out until it had wrapped them both in its embrace.

Jennifer lifted her eyes to his again. "I don't know yet, but I really want to find out."

Jennifer's chest tightened as she waited for Liam to say something more. This was it, the moment she'd both anticipated and dreaded for weeks, maybe for her whole life. Another loud boom racked the car, and golf ball–size droplets pounded the windshield. She twisted her gear shift to set the wipers on max speed, but even that wasn't enough to clear the view. She and Liam were trapped in their own little bubble. Another sign from God?

Liam laughed. "I'm sorry I questioned God's intentions here. Seems like He's making His will pretty obvious."

Jennifer laughed, too. It felt good to let her tension go, to share this light moment with Liam in the middle of their emotionally charged storm.

"It seems weird that we're having this conversation in a cemetery, though," he said, lacing his fingers through hers.

"Creepy weird?" she asked on an exhale.

"Not creepy at all. It's a good weird, I guess. Like, by being here, we somehow have her blessing for . . . whatever happens next."

What would happen next? Would he kiss her, or was it too soon for that? They'd known each other for years, but only well for the past few weeks. Still, she was sure this feeling that swelled in her heart was love —or at least its beginnings. And he was right: Rebecca and God both seemed to approve.

She smiled and turned the radio to a soft rock station to provide a backdrop to their discussion. "Well, you know Rebecca. She never liked to miss out."

"Yes, if I didn't know better, I'd say she orchestrated this whole thing." Liam laughed as he talked about his late wife, but his eyes focused only on Jennifer. His smiles seemed to only be for her in that moment. She didn't know what to expect going into this conversation, but she certainly hadn't anticipated how easy and natural it would feel to talk of her friend and to share her feelings for Liam.

A Kelly Clarkson song started on the radio, bringing with it a memory she decided to share with

Liam. "I remember back in high school, when I was a freshman and Rebecca was a senior, she put together the most amazing senior prank in the entire history of Sweet Grove High. Everyone said she was crazy, that she would for sure get caught and maybe not even be allowed to walk at graduation. But she went ahead with it anyway.

"She, Jessica, and I must have driven all over the state of Texas, buying all the Slip 'N Slides we could find. Rebecca snuck in the night before our final day and lined every single hall with these things. She left these big buckets of sudsy water all over the place so everyone could get wet and wild. And we all did. It was so much fun. To this day, the administrators have no idea what happened."

Liam rested his head back and looked toward the ceiling as they both laughed at the memory. "She was always up for trouble, but her heart was in the right place."

"It was always so exciting with Rebecca, so fun and easy. It's what I loved about her best of all, and when she picked you . . . well, I knew you had to be pretty awesome yourself."

"Same goes for you." He kept his head leaned back but turned to smile at her. "Rebecca never hesitated to make her feelings known, and she raved about you and your sister, your girl nights, everything. I knew you were special to her, but I never knew that one day you'd be special to me, too."

Jennifer nodded. Talking with Liam was becoming easier and easier, more and more natural. She didn't feel embarrassed anymore, only happy. "It came on suddenly, kind of like this rain storm. One minute you're just this guy that my best friend loved, and the next you're the man my thoughts zoom to throughout the day. You're the man who makes me smile whenever you're nearby, and you're the man I want to . . ." She trailed off, realizing this sounded a bit like a marriage proposal. She wanted Liam to know how strongly she felt for him, but not like that!

He sat up straight and hooked an eyebrow at her. "Want to what?"

Okay, now she was a little embarrassed. "I . . . this is all very new to me."

"Relax, I'm just giving you a hard time. The truth is I've only ever been in love once before, but it felt a lot like this." He grabbed both of her hands and held them in his. "I thought I was just lonely or that God was testing me. It felt wrong to move toward happiness again, like by doing that I'd be betraying Rebecca —or worse, forgetting her."

Jennifer swallowed hard. "I could never forget her."

"I know, and that's one of the many reasons that

makes you so perfect for me. I see that now. I'm not sure why I didn't before." He inched closer in his seat. This was happening. Was she ready for it?

"It's like Saul-Paul, right?" she answered, his face so close he must have felt the soft exhale of each syllable. "He was literally blinded by the truth. It took losing his vision to finally see clearly. It's a story I often share with the kids in my class, but I've never experienced for myself until this moment, here with you."

"There's something I need to share with you." He brought a hand to her face and swept her hair from her eyes. "I-I found a letter that Rebecca wrote to Molly Sue before she passed."

Well, that was not what she had expected, but still she wanted to hear more. "What? How?"

"It was folded up in Molly Sue's backpack. It talked about her helping me after Rebecca went to Heaven, talked about being my angel. I think there were more letters, but I couldn't find them."

A lot made sense all of a sudden. "So you think Molly Sue . . . ?"

"I think she knew I liked you before even I did. Somehow, some way, and with her mother's help, no doubt."

She could kiss that little girl, but first she really

wanted to kiss the father. "But how?" she whispered. He was even closer now.

"I don't know." His whispered breath tickled her lips. As much as she wanted him to kiss her, she could have stayed like that in that very moment forever. "But it seems like everyone wants to push us together. Rebecca, Molly Sue, God, who knows who else?"

"And what do you want?" she whispered back.

He stroked her cheek, raised his other hand, and held her face between them. "I don't want to be sad anymore, don't want to be alone. I want to be a good dad for Molly Sue, and I want to do Rebecca's memory proud."

Her brain stopped, just stopped. She only felt, and it felt a lot like love. It felt a lot like forever.

Liam rested his forehead on hers. Their eyelashes brushed as he spoke his next words. "And I think all of those little wants roll up into one very big one. *I want you, Jennifer.*"

She scarcely had a moment to digest his words, because the next thing Jennifer knew, Liam's lips had found hers. And that kiss was like finding a new place she hadn't known existed, a place that already felt like home.

SIXTEEN

Liam woke up the next morning and padded into the kitchen to make a pot of coffee. It had rained all night, and now a bright rainbow stretched over the trees outside his window.

He chuckled. "Okay, God. Enough with the signs already. You've got my attention."

It was Saturday, and he wasn't scheduled to pick up Molly Sue from her friend's house until later that evening. That gave him the whole day to himself. Normally, he would throw himself into work, but today felt like it needed something different.

Today, he had hope—and maybe even love. He had a purpose outside of work.

He had Jennifer.

Last night they had sat together for hours, sharing

their memories of Rebecca and getting to know each other apart from her. They'd kissed once, twice, held hands, and just basked in finally knowing the affection they felt for each other was mutual.

What happened next, he didn't know. But as Jennifer had said, he looked forward to finding out. He felt as if he'd just woken up not only from sleep, but from a fog that had been obscuring his life for nearly two years.

He no longer had to live under a dark cloud. Finally, he could come out and enjoy the sun. And that was exactly what he wanted to do today. Pulling on his long-neglected sneakers, he made quick work of lacing up and headed outside to greet the day.

Rebecca had wanted to settle closer to town, but Liam had insisted on the large, wooded property. He'd always loved nature and regretted not having more of it growing up smack dab in the center of the far too urban Dallas. Out in the woods, a man could be close to his thoughts, close to God, and close to the land, all things he'd been hiding from since the doctor had first delivered Rebecca's grim prognosis.

In that time, Liam had forgotten the things that made him *him*. All that remained was the sadness and the insatiable drive to work, work, work in a half-hearted attempt to give his life some kind of meaning. But inside, the real Liam had never gone away. He'd only waited to be reawakened, and whether it was Jennifer or God or even Molly Sue, someone had finally sounded the alarm.

And he refused to press snooze. Too long he'd waited. Too long he'd been a stranger to himself.

While this revelation grew inside his heart, he walked briskly around the property, taking in all the flowers, weeds, and wildlife that had sprung up in his absence. It seemed trying to distract himself from life's sadness had also caused him to miss out on its beauty. He eyed the dandelions that peppered the far north of his property. They were yellow, Rebecca's favorite color, and while they were weeds, they also had a unique attractiveness.

Weeds had overtaken his life, as well as his lawn. He'd failed to see their beauty then, but there was something satisfying about getting down on your hands and knees and actively working to make something you loved even better.

Like with Molly Sue and her resilience in the face of losing her mother.

And Jennifer's refusal to let life's hardships get her down.

He'd been hiding in the shadows a long time. It was time to greet the sun, time to grow. Weeds would always spring up, no matter what he did to try to stop them, but it was up to him what happened next. He could pluck them out at the roots, plant more flowers, grow, or he could become lost in the tangle.

Liam returned to the garage and found a shovel. It was time to tend the garden.

* * *

J ennifer slept in late that Saturday morning. Her memories of the night before mixed together with sweet, blissful dreams, making her want to stay tucked in her happy cocoon forever. She was back.

She'd let worries consume her too much these past few weeks, and that wasn't like her—not one bit. It seemed as if struggling with her feelings for Liam were at the root of it all, and by denying her true heart's desire—and worse, avoiding God's plan—she'd invited in a host of other problems as well.

Yes, the money problem was tough, but the way she responded to it didn't have to be. Faith in the Lord. His will be done. As she taught the kids in her Sunday school class, *faith it until you make it*. And she'd had the audacity to question God and then complain when things got hard. Not anymore.

God and Rebecca had both given their blessings. Liam and Molly Sue had both let her in, but still Jennifer wanted to make sure she proceeded carefully.

This could be the beginning of her happily ever after. It really could!

She needed advice. Her first thought was to call Jessica, but she would likely be working the weekends as she so often did, and besides, her sister didn't even know Liam. She needed to seek out her best friend on earth, someone who could answer her back, impart some wisdom. And she knew just who that person was.

She threw on jeans and a bunny-patterned blouse, pairing them with a pair of riding boots, then hopped into her car. It hadn't been back from the shop for a week and already the check engine light was aglow. *Never matter*, she told herself. *It will be okay.*

The car made some weird noises, but otherwise did its job of bringing her to Sweet Grove Market.

"Hello!" she sang as she burst through the sliding glass doors. "Hello!" she said again as she barged into Maisie's private office at the front of the store.

Maisie jumped up and hugged her. "You seem happy today!"

"I'm happy every day," Jennifer pointed out.

Maisie cleared her through but didn't argue. "So what's got you happy on *this* day?"

Jennifer gathered a stack of papers from the chair in the corner, then plopped down dramatically. "Love," she said on the wings of a sigh.

"Well, that came out of nowhere." Maisie laughed. "Is it Liam James?"

Jennifer nodded, not bothering to ask how her friend had figured all this out before her big reveal.

"About time," Maisie said with a playful wink. "We all saw that spark at the grand reopening of Mabel's, and we've all seen it at church, too, week after week."

Jennifer slapped her knee in frustration. Well, this was not going how she'd planned. "If you knew already, why didn't you tell me?"

Maisie shrugged. "We knew you knew. You just had to accept it first."

She gave her friend a stern look. "So you all just talked about me and Liam behind my back?"

"Elise did most of the talking for us. I stayed out of it, I swear."

"Well, it's time to get involved, Maisie." Jennifer leaned forward and put her elbows on her legs. "I need your advice."

But Maisie wasn't having it. "Oh my gosh, why are you coming to me for love advice? Remember how I'm single as an ice cream scoop? Talk to Summer. Talk to Kristina Rose. They're the ones with boyfriends. Me? I'm even more clueless than you are!"

Jennifer shook her head and flicked her friend's knee. "It's not about love."

"But you said—"

"It's about *me*. You know me best of all the girls, and besides, you're the smartest, too. Tell me what to do."

Maisie sighed and moved her knee out of flicking range. "What? How could I possibly tell you what to do? I don't know all the details."

"Well, listen up, buttercup, because here they come . . ." Jennifer took a few minutes to recount the weeks of longing, the talk with God, the talk with Liam last night at the cemetery, and their perfect kiss. She ended with, "I don't know what Liam and I are, not exactly, but I think I love him, Maisie. I think this is it."

Her friend sighed, but this time, it was a happy, swoony sigh. "Wow, that's a lot to take in."

"You're telling me."

Maisie fixed a Cheshire grin on her, one that implied she knew something big, something Jennifer hadn't figured out yet. "So do you want me to tell you what to do?"

"Obviously. That's why I'm here!"

Maisie's smile widened as she leaned back in her chair. "Don't do a single thing. Just let love happen. Don't fight it, don't force it, just be open to it. At least that's what I would do if I thought I might have just found my future husband."

Jennifer opened her mouth to argue but stopped when she realized her friend was exactly right, especially that part about future husbands. Could it really be? Could she of all people be on the verge of "I do"?

"Now get out of here! I have work to do, and you have boyfriends to moon over."

"Mmm, just the one, Maisie. Only ever the one."

SEVENTEEN

After his morning spent gardening, Liam prepared a surprise picnic dinner and rehearsed how he'd tell his daughter about what had happened the night before with Jennifer. Would she be excited? Angry? Both? Seeing as she seemed to be rooting for them, it was hard to picture her feeling anything but happy. Still, this was a sensitive situation —one he'd never been in before—and he needed to treat it delicately. The picnic would help, at the very least.

When at last he picked Molly Sue up that afternoon, it felt as if he hadn't seen her for days. So much had happened during her short sleepover.

"Hey, kiddo. I've got a surprise for you," he said when they returned home. "Go look in the fridge."

Molly Sue dropped her overnight bag on the floor and ran toward the kitchen. As soon as her footsteps quieted, he heard a squeal of delight. "A picnic? Oh, Daddy, you're the best!" She slammed the fridge closed and ran back out to meet him. "I have to put on my Anna dress," she shouted with glee. "I'll be right back!"

"I'll work on getting us set up on the lawn. Come outside when you're all changed!" he shouted after her.

"It's too bad you don't have a Kristoff outfit," Molly Sue said as she took her seat on the checked blanket a few minutes later. "Then we would match. And you know what else?"

"What?" He loved seeing his daughter this excited. Maybe she'd be happy about his news, too. Maybe this whole evening would be straight out of one of her fairytale movies.

"We should think about getting a reindeer." She laughed and then sang, "Reindeers are better than people!"

"You can't go five seconds without making a Disney reference, can you?" He laughed, but it didn't bother her a bit.

"Nope. Hey, did you make sandwiches, Daddy? That's Anna's favorite."

"Sure did." He pulled the carefully packed

containers of food from their basket, starting first with the turkey BLTs he'd prepared just for the occasion.

"With bacon? My favorite!" Molly Sue dug in, unaware mayonnaise glopped onto her dress as she took one big bite after the next.

"Why aren't you eating?" she asked, nudging the container back toward him.

"I will, but first I have something important I need to talk with you about."

"Uh-oh." She wiped her mouth with the back of her hand and looked up at him, worry hiding behind her eyes. "Am I in trouble?"

"No, no, nothing like that. It's a good thing, I think. I just don't know how to tell you about it."

"Like a Band-Aid, Daddy. *Rip!*" She mimed the gesture, keeping her eyes fixed on him the whole time.

"A Band-Aid, huh?"

She nodded encouragingly.

"Okay, here goes nothing." He took a deep breath, and then let it all out at once. "I found a letter from your mom in your backpack, talking about being my angel. I didn't understand at first, but now I think I do."

Molly Sue's lower lip trembled. "Oh no, I—"

"No, it's okay! Just let me finish. I think you and

your mom were trying to fix me up, and I think it worked. Last night, Miss Elliott and I decided to—"

"Miss Elliott? Oh, I knew it would be her! You kissed her, didn't you, Daddy? Just like Eric and Ariel in *The Little Mermaid*." And now she was singing another Disney song, puckering her lips in a smooching gesture between lines.

"Not that it's any of your business, but yes." He smiled and ran his sweaty palms over his knees. "I really like her, Molly Sue. I *like her* like her."

She shot forward and wrapped her arms around him in a tight hug. "I knew it! I knew it! I knew it!"

She leaned back with a triumphant look in her eyes, then popped to her feet. "I'll be right back!"

Molly Sue and Liam
Present day

It was finally happening, just the way Mommy had said it would. Molly Sue ran across the yard and up to her bedroom. There, tucked in her Elsa castle, she found the letters she had stowed away more than a year ago. She flipped through them all excitedly, remembering to put one aside. That one wasn't meant to be shared with Daddy. The rest, though, could finally come out. Molly Sue had kept the secret for a very long time, and it felt good to get it off her chest once and for all. She felt so light, like she could float all the way to Heaven, just from the fullness of her heart.

She'd finished her job. She'd helped Daddy as Mommy had asked. Now there didn't have to be any more secrets or important job. Now she could just be a kid again, and Daddy could be himself again, too.

She tucked the last letter into the hiding place inside her castle and ran back outside with the rest to show Daddy.

"I knew it!" he shouted and ran to pick her up and hug her tight. "Your mom left more letters for you. May I read them?"

He placed Molly Sue back into the springy grass, and they returned to their picnic blanket.

"She left a letter for you, too," she said, handing him the first of the letters.

Tears filled Daddy's eyes. She hadn't seen him cry since Mommy died. Usually, he sucked the tears back inside and went away so Molly Sue wouldn't see how sad he felt. This time, though, the tears fell on his cheeks and rolled down onto the checkered blanket like big, fat raindrops.

"Daddy, if you cry like that, you won't be able to read the letter," she pointed out.

He chuckled and choked back a sob. "You're right. Will you read it to me?"

"Are you sure? I don't want to make you cry."

"Well, now you have to read it to me. Besides, these are happy tears. Hearing from your mom after she's been gone a full year, it's like the most special gift I could ever receive."

"Okay, if you promise they're happy tears." Molly Sue unfolded the letter, took a deep breath, and read.

My dearest Liam,

So Molly Sue finally gave you this letter? I knew it would take a while, but I'm so glad you are finally moving forward with your life. I'm writing because I'm worried about you. I'm not worried about our daughter, because I know you will do a great job taking care of her when I go. But I do worry for you, Liam. I worry so deeply. Who will take care of you when I go away?

I know how easy it is to lose yourself in the sadness, how easy it is to get stuck—especially for you, because you're so stubborn. That's why I asked our daughter to prod you along and get you moving forward again. I asked her to pay attention, to watch and wait, and be your angel. Specifically, I asked her to be your cupid.

Liam, you're a young man. Your life isn't over just because mine is. I want you—need you—to keep living for the both of us. Find joy again, be happy, and more than anything, let love into your heart. Don't feel guilty, unless you completely ignore my advice, then you should *feel very guilty. Man was not made to live alone, and neither are you.*

You need a partner. Our daughter needs a mother, and neither are roles I can actively play from Heaven. Make this family whole again, Liam. You have my permission; it's okay. Please don't put me on such a high pedestal that no other woman is ever good enough again. I had lots of flaws! Remember how I burned the lasagna every single time I tried to make it from your mother's recipe? And how I forgot to pick up Molly Sue from preschool on more than one occasion? See? Lots of flaws.

We are all broken just a little bit, Liam, but we're not shattered. We're like puzzle pieces. Our family is like a puzzle with a missing piece, and when a piece goes missing, it ruins the whole picture. You can't help but stare at the hole, at what's missing. Find a new piece, make a new picture. It's time.

Liam, I love you so much. That will never change. And I know you'll never stop loving me, but the time has come to open your heart wider, to let more love in. Keep your love for me, but also give your love to somebody else, someone deserving, kind, and most of all, someone who knows how lucky she is to have you and Molly Sue in her life.

You two are my everything, dear. Now it's time to make someone new the luckiest woman this side of Heaven. Molly Sue gave you this letter now because she believes you've found the perfect person.

Stop wondering what I would have wanted. I have always wanted you to be happy and to live a life of love.

Let love back in. It's time.

Your Rebecca

EIGHTEEN

Liam leaned back on his palms and watched as his daughter read the words his wife had left for him. He'd expected to cry harder and harder, but instead his tears dried up, and he laughed. And laughed. And laughed.

Molly Sue scrunched up her nose and looked at him like he was crazy. Perhaps he was.

"Thank you," he told Molly Sue. "Thank you!" he shouted to Rebecca in Heaven.

"Why are you laughing?"

He did his best to explain between deep gulps of air. "I feel like it's all the laughs I kept bottled up, and now that they're coming out, they don't want to stop."

"That's weird, Daddy. Don't do that in front of

Miss Elliott or she won't want to kiss you anymore." Now Molly Sue laughed with him, but probably for different reasons.

He tried to sober up but couldn't help it. He and his daughter laughed together for what felt like ages, and it was almost like a miracle.

"So you knew all along?" he asked when they had both laid back on the checkered blanket to look up at the clouds.

Molly Sue pointed out a heart-shaped cloud as it breezed by. "Mommy didn't say who the special lady would be, only that I'd know when she came."

"And how did you know it was Jennifer?"

She turned her head to look at him. "Because you smiled again and meant it."

There were tears, and he wasn't sure whether they were from the laughter or from something else. His poor little girl had been forced to endure so much in her short life, and she'd handled it with the grace of an angel. His angel.

He rubbed his fingers on her cheek until she smiled, too. "Now that my smile is back, I won't let it go away again. I promise."

"Does this mean you don't feel sad about Mommy anymore? That you don't miss her?" she asked in a small, broken voice.

"Not at all. Sit with me, kiddo." He sat up,

slapped his knee, and invited her to sit in his lap, something they hadn't done for a very long time.

"I still love your mom and miss her every single day, but I also understand now that she doesn't want me to mope—doesn't want you to, either. Your mommy loved to laugh. She loved to be happy. And by being happy ourselves, we are remembering and honoring her. Does that make sense?"

"I think so. So now that you are happy, does that mean we're all going to live happily ever after like in my movies?"

He laughed, careful not to get lost in his merriment again. "C'mon now, that would be too easy. You know real life isn't like the movies. We aren't guaranteed a happily ever after, but still we go on living our lives, trying our best to get one. It's what God wants for all of us, and there's no doubt in my mind that God helped you and your mom with your plan to bring Jennifer into our lives."

"It's weird for you to call Miss Elliott 'Jennifer,' Daddy." She scrunched up her nose, a sure sign she had something deep on her mind. At last, Molly Sue asked, "Is she going to be my new mommy now?"

"Not now. I like Miss Elliott, maybe even love her, but grown-ups need time to figure out if their lives fit together before committing to each other in that way."

Her eyes lit up and she sat straighter. "Time? Like time together? Like a date?"

"Yeah, exactly."

"So what are you doing here with me? You need to take Miss Elliott on a date!" She hopped to her feet and paced the length of the blanket.

"Okay, seeing as you've already made my love life your business, tell me. What should we do for our first date?"

"That's easy. You need to make her feel like a princess."

"Oh, that's easy, huh? Why didn't I think of it?"

Jennifer didn't see Liam again until after Sunday's service. When he arrived to pick up Molly Sue from her class, he pulled her aside, a mischievous smile on his face.

"I hope you haven't made plans for lunch or brunch or anything else, because I was hoping you could come out to my place today," he said quietly, but not quietly enough to prevent a few onlookers.

She caught Elise's eye across the room and shooed her away, then smiled up at Liam. "That depends. Would this be like a date?"

"Not *like* a date. A date, period." He ran a hand

through his hair in an *aw shucks* move. "Yes, please date me."

They both chuckled, and she leaned in to give him a hug. "I do have one condition."

"Name it."

Jennifer saw her friends gather across the foyer but quickly turned her focus back so it was all on the handsome man standing before her. "Can I ride with you and Molly Sue? My car is giving me a fresh set of troubles, and I'd rather not break down in the middle of the woods. You know, if it can be avoided."

"Oh, is that all?" He let out a slow breath. "I was worried it would be something much harder than that. Of course you can ride with us. In fact, I insist that you do. Are you ready to go?"

"Yup!" She tried not to skip with delight as she went to grab her purse and jacket. *An actual date with Liam! I can't believe it!* She said a few more goodbyes, then followed Molly Sue and Liam out to the parking lot.

"Hi, Miss Elliott," the little girl said, even though they'd just spent the last hour and a half together. "You look really pretty today."

"Thank you. So do you," she called over her shoulder as she took a seat in the front and Molly Sue climbed into the back.

"Daddy said I could come on the first part of

your date, but after that, my friend's mom is going to come pick me up and take me away. Then you can have alone grown-up time."

Jennifer was glad that Molly Sue couldn't see the expression of shock and embarrassment that must have shot across her face in that moment.

"She doesn't mean it like that," Liam said with a laugh.

"Like what, Daddy?"

Jennifer risked a glance back and saw Molly Sue cock her head to the side like a curious puppy.

"Never mind," Liam answered firmly. "Hey, should I put on the playlist you made for us?"

Jennifer grabbed onto the topic change with both hands. "You made us a playlist, Molly Sue? What's on it?"

The little girl nodded proudly. "It's all the best Disney love songs," she explained as "Can You Feel the Love Tonight?" started playing through the surround sound speakers.

"Oh, I love *The Lion King*," Jennifer gushed.

About a half hour later, they pulled up to Liam's house, and it was larger than Jennifer had remembered. What took her most by surprise, though, was the fact her bike was propped neatly up against the porch. It looked like it had been given a spit shine, too.

"What's this?" she asked, not sure what else to say.

"Sorry, I kind of stole your bike last night so we could all go riding today." Liam smirked, then turned away. "Hang on."

Molly Sue ran inside the garage and pushed her bike out by the handlebars. At least, Jennifer thought it was a bike. It was hard to tell underneath all the added dressings.

"It's a unicorn bike!" Molly Sue cried, ringing the bell.

Liam returned, too, pushing his bike with one hand and carrying something shiny in the other.

"It's a tiara!" Molly Sue squealed, pointing to Jennifer's head and then her own. "So you can be a princess! See, my helmet has a crown on it, too."

Jennifer bent down as Liam fixed the dainty crown in her hair. "How do I look?" she asked when he'd finished.

"Like a princess," he and Molly Sue said in unison.

They rode for hours in and out of the woods and the deserted roads north of town. As they journeyed, Molly Sue sang her favorite Disney songs, inviting Liam and Jennifer to join her for the ones they knew. They stopped off at the house for a quick meal somewhere in between, then went out riding again. It felt so good to ride her bike simply for the joy of it, and it felt even better to be carefree and happy like a kid again—especially with Liam riding right beside her.

So they pedaled hard and sang loud, riding into the twilight. They made it home just as darkness had begun to fall. A green van idled in the driveway.

Molly Sue carefully returned her bike to the garage and then gave both Liam and Jennifer tight hugs. "I had the best time today. Thank you," she told Jennifer.

"Hey, that's supposed to be my line." Jennifer laughed.

"I have to go to my friend's now." She pointed toward the van. "But I hope you'll enjoy the next part of the date. No matter what Daddy says, it was actually all my idea."

The little girl skipped away into the waiting van, leaving Jennifer and Liam alone for the first time since their heart-to-heart on Friday night.

He hummed one of Molly Sue's songs from their ride and twirled Jennifer in a dance, then leaned in and pressed his mouth to hers.

"*That* was Molly Sue's idea?" she asked after they both came up for air.

"No, that was all mine." He raised his eyebrows at her in an endearing and sexy display. "Mind if I steal another kiss?"

She gasped. "Never."

He swept Jennifer off her feet and lifted her into his arms, then kissed her again.

Liam walked her over to the porch and set her on the steps. "Be right back."

When he returned, he had a new crown for her —this one made of flowers—and a large shopping bag.

"What's all this?" she asked with a giggle.

"Molly Sue thought we should recreate one of her favorite Disney movie scenes. You'll be playing the part of Rapunzel."

She hadn't seen *Tangled* as much as the older Disney princess movies, but she was pretty sure she knew how this would go. "Which would make you . . . ?"

"Flynn Ryder, at your service." Liam gave an exaggerated bow, then helped her switch crowns.

She rolled her eyes at him but secretly loved it, loved him, loved everything about this day. "I hate to break it to you, but my hair is not magic."

"That's okay. I have a different kind of magic." He flashed a lighter, then unpacked the rest of the bag, laying everything out across the porch planks.

"The lanterns," she said as a breeze swept across the yard.

"Yup. Oh, that reminds me. I promised Molly Sue I'd play the *Tangled* soundtrack for this." He dropped his iPhone into a speaker and music started to play.

"Just like Rebecca was part of our first kiss, and Molly Sue was part of our first date, I wanted to bring God in as well. I mean, He helped in a big way, right?"

Jennifer nodded and hugged her knees to her chest as the night chill began to set in.

Liam brandished a marker. "Before we release the lanterns, I figured we could both write down a prayer, then send them up to Heaven." His eyes shone in the setting sun. "Mine will be a prayer of thanks."

He moved closer to her and put an arm over her shoulders, and she rested her head on his arm and sighed. "This is perfect. Thank you."

They sat like that for a while. She enjoyed the feel of his arms around her, the comfort in the silence as their hearts matched tempo. When the sun had completed its descent, she said, "Do you mind if I write a message to Rebecca instead?"

"Not at all. Are you ready?" He smiled. Things were so natural now that they were no longer fighting it. Perhaps she owed God a prayer of thanks, too, but she would make sure to do that later tonight. For now, she knew exactly what she needed to say and who it needed to be said to.

Liam handed her a marker, and she wrote:

Rebecca, I promise to honor your memory and to take care of them both. Forever your friend, Jennifer

And when they released the lanterns into the sky, she watched until she could no longer discern the lanterns from the stars, or the wishes of her heart with the new reality of her life.

NINETEEN

Liam hated dropping Jennifer off after their date. She belonged here with him, and taking her away was a new form of torture in his otherwise far happier existence. Still, he needed time to get things ready, to make things right.

Molly Sue's friend's mom had agreed to see her to school the next day, which meant the night was all his. Time to continue the work he'd started a few weeks prior, especially now that he knew just what he needed to do.

He worked late into the night, then woke up early and worked several hours more. This didn't mean the old Liam was back and hiding from the world. In fact, shortly after lunch, he made the half-hour drive over to Jennifer's apartment to surprise her with a visit.

"Liam!" She hurled herself into his arms the moment he opened the door. "What are you doing here? I mean, I'm super happy to see you, but don't you have work, mister?"

"I'm here," he answered, giving her a quick kiss, "because I wanted to see my girlfriend."

"But work?" *Wait, why am I trying to convince him he shouldn't be here? I love that he's here!*

"I work too much," he said with a dismissive wave. "Besides, lately I've been spending the bulk of my time just spinning wheels and doing busy work, things I can offload onto someone else."

"Does that mean you . . . ?" She followed as he strode into the living room and plopped onto the couch.

"Hired an assistant? You betcha." He winked at her, then laughed before explaining more. "Her name is Angi, and she's fresh out of business school. She's smart as a whip, full of energy, and I trust her fully."

Jennifer leaned forward in her seat and frowned. "She sounds great. Hey, should I be jealous?"

"Not one bit," he answered, pulling her to his chest, a place she'd recently found she fit perfectly against. "Would it make you feel better to know she's a virtual assistant?"

"I'm just giving you a hard time. I'm glad you're here. Last night was . . ."

"Amazing," they said together.

"It was, and it's a big part of the reason I came to see you today." He sighed and gave her a quick kiss on the forehead before standing once again. "But, sadly, it's not the only reason."

"Uh-oh. What's going on?"

"I'm not sure how long it will take, so I need to get to work."

"But I thought you hired Angi so you could stop working as much as you do?"

"That's my *job*. This is . . . well, as your boyfriend, it's kind of my job, too."

She still had no idea what he was talking about, and apparently her expression conveyed her confusion enough for him to explain himself before he opened the door and headed back outside.

"I'm going to fix your car once and for all."

"Oh no, you don't have to do that. It'll be fine." She chased after him, but he was determined as he strode down the stairs and toward the parking lot.

"No, I don't like worrying about you. What if you broke down in the woods?"

"We could take it to Tom Hanson." She hated pointing this out, but money pretty much grew on trees for Liam James—and he had plenty of trees. "If you're that worried, you could lend me the money and—"

"Not the point. Too often I've waved a wad of cash in place of putting in the time. With Rebecca. With Molly Sue. And I want to start our relationship off right." He stopped suddenly and she thudded into his back, causing them both to laugh as he turned and wrapped her in his arms. "Jennifer, I'm fixing your car. But I wouldn't argue if you wanted to come keep me company."

"Anywhere you're going, I want to go, too. But I gotta tell you, I'm useless when it comes to stuff like this."

"Oh, believe me, I won't be asking you to so much as find the right wrench. I just want to be with you, and I want to take care of you. Is that okay?"

She stood on tiptoe and pressed a kiss to his lips in response. It felt so good, so right, to finally just relax and let someone who cared about her help.

"I take it that's a yes," he joked. "Now c'mon. If we pause to kiss every few feet, we'll never make it to your parking space before midnight."

* * *

Jennifer watched as Liam lowered himself onto the cold pavement. He looked so out of place in his finely tailored clothes that probably cost more than her entire car, but she loved that he was trying so hard to support her.

"Can I get you a blanket or something?" she asked.

"Nah, a little dirt never hurt anybody," he answered as he pushed himself under the car.

She worried at her lip, trying not to be overly protective, but her car had to weigh at least a ton, and she wasn't ready to lose Liam now that she'd finally found him. "Is it safe?"

"Totally safe," his muffled answer came out from under the carriage. "That's why we jacked it up and secured it before I got started."

"But it *is* my car we're talking about. It has a way of doing the unexpected."

"I'm sure I can manage," he said. "Now, can you hand me that flashlight?"

"You said you wouldn't ask me to hand you stuff," she joked, retrieving the light and sliding it under the car to his outstretched hand.

"That was the last time, I swear," he answered, and she could hear the smile in his words. From never smiling to always wearing a grin now. Just as he'd helped her, it seemed she'd helped him as well. That's what happened when you followed the plan God set out for you. Good, good things.

"Good afternoon, there!" someone said from across the lot.

Jennifer pivoted toward the familiar voice. "Oh, Dave, hi! Liam, it's Dave!"

"Hi, Dave," he grunted from beneath the car.

"Got anything good for me today?" she asked the mailman.

"Probably not, but here, take a look." Dave handed her a bundle of letters and flyers secured with a rubber band.

"Thanks."

"You're welcome. I'll just be on my way. Nice seeing you, Jennifer. Liam." Dave nodded and dismissed himself to place the rest of the building's mail inside the assigned cubbies.

She thumbed through her mail. *Bill, bill, bill, what else is new?*

"Did you fix it yet?" she asked Liam as she searched through the stack. "I want to go in and spend time with you."

"Hold your horses. I'm still looking for the problem. Well, make that *problems.* I've already found a couple. It's a wonder this thing runs at all."

"Yeah, that's what Tom Hanson said, too." She pulled out a coupon circular for Sweet Grove Market, and a thick letter fluttered down to the pavement.

"Oh!" she cried in surprise.

"What is it?" Liam pulled himself out from under the car and wiped his hands on a rag.

"A letter from my sister Jessica."

"Are you going to open it?"

"Hold your horses," she quipped back as she tore into the letter. There wasn't much to read, just three short handwritten lines.

Look.

   Already paid for.

   Now you have to come!

And with the note were a pair of tickets, one for a plane and one for Disneyland.

"Hey." Liam wrapped his arms around her from behind and nuzzled her neck. "You didn't tell me you were going to Disney this spring. Molly Sue will be so jealous."

"I didn't know I was until just now," she confessed. That Jessica always found a way to get what she wanted, but would it really be so bad to take a vacation and catch up with her family? The only problem would be . . .

She spun to face Liam, so excited she could hardly get the words out fast enough. "Hey, you two should come with us!"

"Oh, I didn't mean to intrude. I just meant—"

"No, you have to come! My nieces, Kelsey and Jamie, are about Molly Sue's age. The girls would all have so much fun together. Besides, I'd miss you way too much if I had to leave you behind for a full week."

"Well, if we have to." He laughed before repeating her words from earlier. "Besides, anywhere you're going, I want to go, too. Um, just check with your sister first, maybe?"

"I'll go call her now. Give you some alone time with my old rust bucket there."

"That is an apt name for it."

"Oh, shut up and let me go call." She playfully hit him on the chest with the pile of mail, and he pretended the blow was much harder than it had been. "You're so dramatic," she teased, "and I'm so excited!"

And she really was. Now even her sister had a role to play in the great love story unfolding in her life.

She needed to stop questioning the author of her and Liam's story and finally just go along with the plot.

She couldn't wait to see what happened next.

TWENTY

"Are we really going to Disneyland? Honest?" Molly Sue asked with reverence when Liam told her the news.

"We really, honestly are. I mean, that is, if you want to go."

"Daddy, I have been waiting my whole life for this," she said, pacing back and forth excitedly now.

He hooked an eyebrow at her and tried not to laugh. "All seven years, huh?" The irony seemed to be lost on her. "You're going to have to wait another couple of months, though," he pointed out. "Think you can manage?"

"Yes, yes, yes," Molly Sue said quickly as she continued to pace and spin around the room. "That will give us enough time to get our outfits ready. We have to pick some for you, too."

"And for Miss Elliott," he said, watching as his daughter's wave of energy suddenly ebbed.

She stood stock-still as she took the news in, but then her eyes danced and a giant smile cha-cha'd from one chubby cheek to the other. "Do you really, honestly mean it?"

"I do," he answered, wondering when he might get a chance to say these words again next. There was one thing he knew beyond the shadow of a doubt, and that was that he loved Jennifer Elliott with his whole heart.

"Oh, Daddy, I am so happy!" Molly Sue squealed.

"Me, too, Molly Sue. Me, too." She jumped into his arms, and they hugged with happiness, relief, and maybe a bit of extra hope, too.

"Mommy's letters, they really worked. Didn't they?" Molly Sue asked, breathless from all the excitement.

"More than her letters—it was you." He tucked her hair behind her ears, noting how much she looked like her mother these days. "You know that, don't you?"

She shrugged. "I guess, but I feel kind of sad that I'm done helping people now. At first I was excited to go back to being a kid, but now that I know how happy it can make others to help when they need it, I want to keep doing it."

"Well, it's true you're done helping me with this now, but I'm kind of a screwup sometimes. I'll bet you'll find plenty more ways to help me if you just give it time, and if that's not soon enough, I think I have another idea."

* * *

A few months later

Molly Sue raced down the hall the moment she heard the doorbell and threw herself into Jennifer's waiting arms. Over the last couple of months, she'd stopped thinking of her as Miss Elliott —but calling her Jennifer wasn't exactly right either.

"Are you ready for Disneyland, little miss?" Jennifer asked, using the new nickname she'd given her.

"Sure am! Daddy and I finished the last of the bottles this morning." It had been Daddy's idea to write notes of encouragement and place them into old bottles that they would then toss into the ocean on the edge of California. That way, Molly Sue could write letters that helped people, too. Molly Sue hoped and prayed that one of her messages would land all the way in China. How cool would it be to help someone on the whole way opposite side of the world?

Mommy's letters had changed their lives: hers, Daddy's, and Jennifer's. Maybe Molly Sue's letters could change somebody's life, too.

Molly knew for a definite, honest fact that Jennifer was the one Mommy had prepared them for, and that's why she'd saved the last of Mommy's letters to give to Jennifer today.

"Can you come with me to my room please?" she asked, trying not to act suspiciously. The letter was meant for Jennifer and only Jennifer, and she didn't want Daddy following them upstairs.

When they'd made it safely to her room, she shut the door and even locked it—something she almost never did.

"What's up?" Jennifer asked. She looked a little worried.

"I have something for you," she said, running over to Elsa's castle and taking out the last of Mommy's letters. "It's from my mom."

Jennifer gasped as she unfolded the letter.

"Go ahead and read it," Molly Sue nudged. "I already know what it says, which is why I wanted to give it to you."

Jennifer's hands shook as she held the letter.

Molly Sue watched her eyes go back and forth, back and forth, all the way to the end.

The letter said:

Hello, you. It's funny I don't know how to address this letter. I don't even know who you are, but I know your heart. Because your heart and my heart beat for the same handsome man and smart little girl. The fact that you're reading this letter means that Molly Sue believes you are the perfect person to complete our family.

I know it won't be easy, coming in after I've gone. And I apologize in advance for that. But I do not want you to feel guilty. I'm not jealous, not upset, not at all. In fact, you're my hero. My daughter needs a mother to guide her through life, to teach her about boys, and to dry her tears when they break her heart. She needs someone to root for her, to teach her, to love her.

And Liam needs you even more. When I died, a big part of him joined me in the grave. I know it, because I saw him slipping away even before the end. He's hurting and scared, angry with God. He's forgotten that light exists because he feels trapped in the dark.

But you, you can bring brightness to his world again, give him a new chance. I hate that he feels the need to keep his candle burning only for me even though I'm no longer there to light the match. He needs a partner to share his life, and that is something I am unable to do from this side of Heaven.

Liam is a good man, a man who knows how to love. Help him remember that. Please show him that by loving you, he does not need to stop loving me. Please help him understand that I want him to open his heart again. It's the only way I know he and Molly Sue will be okay.

I have another favor to ask, too. Please remind him that God is good, remind him of the unshakeable faith he once had. For it is only by loving God that we are truly able to love others, and you and Molly Sue both deserve all of Liam's heart, not just the piece that hasn't broken.

I told Molly Sue that she is her daddy's angel, but did you know you're an angel, too? You, a woman I don't know, who I may have never even met—you are my angel. Because of *your grace and goodness, because of your capacity to love, I can close my eyes one last time and know that everything is taken care of.*

Thank you for loving my daughter. Thank you for loving Liam. I will not call him "my husband," though he was, because I am hoping that someday soon perhaps he can be your husband, too. Molly Sue is a very smart little girl. She would not have given you my letter unless she truly saw love shine between you and Liam.

If he hasn't said it yet to you, allow me to say it in his place. He loves you. Molly Sue loves you, and I, I love you, too. You are my hero, my angel, you are everything I ever wanted for them.

I will thank you in person one day when we meet at the pearly gates. Please take care of your new family and know that we are all so blessed that you have entered their lives. I hope the blessings return to you tenfold, and I wish you the happily ever after I never quite got to finish.

Your friend in Christ,
Rebecca James

"Are you finished yet?" Molly Sue asked when she noticed that Jennifer's eyes were focused on a single spot at the bottom of the page.

"Thank you for giving this to me," Jennifer whispered. "It helps so much."

Molly Sue nodded and wrapped her arms around Jennifer's legs. "Mommy would have been so happy to know that it's you."

"Molly Sue, thank you. That means the world to me."

"May I ask you a favor?"

"Of course, anything." Jennifer wiped at tears that had formed at the edges of her eyes as she waited for Molly Sue to say more.

There was only one thing left to say. "Will you please marry us?"

* * *

Jennifer stumbled back until her legs met Molly Sue's bed, then she sunk down in disbelief. "Did your dad tell you to ask me that?"

The little girl shook her head adamantly. "No, but I want you to ask him."

"To marry me?"

"Yes, please." Molly Sue grinned from ear to ear,

either not knowing or not caring that this wasn't exactly how marriage proposals were done.

"Molly Sue, it's not that simple. Grown-ups need to—"

Molly Sue grabbed both of Jennifer's wrists and looked her straight in the eyes. "Do you love him?"

"More than anything. It's just that I—"

"And do you want to marry him?"

There was only one answer to give. "Yes."

"Then do it already!" she huffed, throwing her arms up. "Grown-ups are so silly. They wait too long for everything. You belong here with us, but to live in our house, you have to marry Daddy. Maybe you could get married at Disneyland, that way when we come home, you can stay!"

"I think that maybe—"

"And then you can have babies! I would love a little brother, but I would be okay with a sister, too."

"Molly Sue!" she hissed, then couldn't help but laugh at the earnestness in Molly's expression.

The little girl smiled at her, and Jennifer knew she was looking into the face of her daughter. She also knew that she would find happily ever after a little sooner than expected, but hey, that was life for you, and that's what made it so wonderful to live.

EPILOGUE

Sally Scott clicked her pen, then clicked it again and again, creating a steady beat to serve as the backdrop to her thoughts. The library had cleared out a few minutes back, which meant she had a bit of precious time to herself. Well, to her story, really.

Nobody in town knew she dreamed of one day seeing her name at the top of the *New York Times* Best Sellers list, and she preferred to keep it that way. Even if her neighbors did find out about her writerly ambition, they probably wouldn't care anyway. At least not until she proved herself to the greater world first.

Before that, though, she needed to get the words onto the paper, to bring the characters to life so that one day—when she was ready—they could be shared with others. She loved escaping into her fantasy realm, a world where she made the rules and her dreams actually came true. She'd spent hours poring over both Tolkien and Shakespeare to make sure her work was grounded in not just one but two proud literary traditions.

Her hero, Benneth, made Aragorn and Oberon look like bald dwarves by comparison, with wit to rival the mischievous Puck. Yes, Benneth had everything a good hero needed, from sandy hair and striking green eyes down to a sensitive soul and willingness to travel to the ends of the earth for the one he loved.

In her novel, that lucky heroine was Salin, an intelligent scribe who worked on the kingdom's annals. Salin had fair skin, dark hair, and often found herself overlooked by the nobility and peasants alike, but she had Benneth's heart, and that was everything she needed anyway.

Okay, okay, so maybe her story had been based somewhat in her own reality. She couldn't argue that she'd used herself as a model for Salin. And Benneth? Well, he bore a few crucial resemblances to Ben Davis, the only person she'd ever loved since she first set eyes on him in kindergarten.

But Benneth had been tricked by the evil fairy enchantress in disguise, and now he was due to be wed to that same villainess known only as Solstice. Unfortunately, that part had been based in reality, too. Sweet Grove Ben was engaged to be married to Sweet Grove Summer, and there wasn't a thing Sweet Grove Sally could do about it. Salin from the land of Lophased, though, would not be defeated so easily.

"Sally! There you are!" Ben shouted, rushing up to her large, circular desk in the center of the library.

"Well, where else would I be, Ben?" she said, delighting in the taste of his name on her tongue. "Also, we're in a library, so shhhh."

"Oh, sorry." When he smiled at her, she melted a little. So many smiles over the years, it was a small wonder Sally hadn't completely turned into a puddle at his feet.

"Hey, what's that you've got there?" he asked, reaching out to take her spiral-bound notebook, the same one that held her story. "Can I see that?"

"You most certainly cannot," she snapped.

"Oh, sorry. I didn't mean to . . ." He crimsoned. "Anyway, did you hear the news?"

The news, *ugh*. Sally had hated the news ever since Ben's fiancée Summer Smith had taken over the local paper. In fact, she actively avoided the news. It was just not fair that somehow this new neighbor had managed to win both Sally's one true love and the only paid writing gig in town. Not fair at all.

She put on a smile. She would never earn a come-from-behind victory in the race for Ben's heart if she sat here with a scowl on her face the whole day. "You seem pretty excited about it. Tell me what's going on."

He took a deep breath and then shouted again, "They did it! Jennifer and Liam actually did it!"

"Did what? And, seriously, library, remember?"

Ben continued on, only a couple of notches quieter than before. "They got married!"

"Married? What? Are you sure? Last I heard they'd gone to Disneyland for spring break."

"That's what I'm trying to tell you. They eloped, and they did it at Cinderella's castle! Can you believe it?" he asked breathlessly.

No, she honestly could not. Jennifer Elliott. Now *there* was another woman who had unfairly found her happily ever after before Sally—and at a fantasy castle, no less. It was like all of Sally's wishes and dreams went to God's ears, only to disappear into the ether. When would Sally's prince come? When would he realize the only one who would ever truly under-stand him had been right here this whole time? Had been ready and waiting for him to see that, yes, the shoe fit and she wanted to wear it?

"Anyway," Ben continued on, "Summer and I are taking the lead on planning a big reception for them. I was wondering if you could help by printing off some invitations. It wouldn't be the same without you there."

"Of course," she said aloud, mentally adding, *I'd do anything for you.*

"Great! I've still got some more errands to run, but I'll come by again in a couple of hours. See you soon?"

"I'll be here." Waiting, always waiting.

Sally watched as Ben retreated through the double doors of the old library. He was always doing that—going away, leaving her to be someplace else.

Maybe it was time Sally did that, too. Time was running out. If Ben and Summer did say "I do" come May, there would be nothing left for her in Sweet Grove.

But would she really be able to convince him that she'd been his perfect match all along?

Ben and Summer's wedding is fast approaching. Will it go off without a hitch? *Love's Vow* **will be here August 8. Learn more or preorder your copy at www.MelStorm.com/Vow.**

Love is patient . . . It's been nearly a year since Ben Davis first laid eyes on Summer Smith, the woman who would be his saving grace. Now, on the eve of their wedding, the entire town of Sweet Grove is in chaos. The wedding garden never bloomed, the flower girl has the flu, and the ring bearer won't stop biting everyone!

Love is kind . . . Ben's father is back in town for the first time in years and has brought his new wife and family with him, testing the limits of Susan's recovery. Meanwhile, both the maid of honor and the pastor are stuck out of town and may not even make it to the ceremony in time. And if diner matriarch Mabel refuses to take her retirement seriously, she just may end up at the hospital instead of the wedding reception.

Love never fails. It's First Street Church's first wedding of the season, and nothing is going as planned. Can this small Texas town pull together to give Ben and Summer a wedding they'll never forget?

Don't miss another chance to visit the close-knit community of Sweet Grove—get your copy of Love's Vow today at www.MelStorm.com/vow.

ACKNOWLEDGMENTS

Wow, I ran the entire gamut of emotions when writing this book. I smiled at Molly Sue's innocence, especially considering many of her interests and quirks were based off those of my own little girl, Phoenix Ruby Storm. I swooned as Jennifer and Liam found their way to each other and swooned when my husband, Falcon, helped me plan their very special Disney date. That beautiful lantern scene? It came from the mind of my own Mr. Happily Ever After!

So, of course, I must thank my family first and foremost, and that includes the child we'll soon be adopting from Bulgaria, the little boy or girl I haven't even met yet. It includes my parents, siblings, cousins, and—most of all—a very special aunt and uncle who, as a certain Molly Sue James would say, mean a whole very lot to me.

My aunt Cindy and uncle Darryl Powlison served as that first spark of inspiration for Liam and Jennifer's story. My aunt was actually friends with my uncle's first wife, who—like Rebecca—died young of cancer. The biggest reason, though, that this story is for them is because I first recognized true love when I saw the way they looked at each other. Even as a child, I could see how pure and full their hearts were for each other, and they kept that love burning bright as a beacon of hope and faith, even amid the darkness of the liver disease that would eventually take him. They never stopped celebrating their love, never stopped appreciating each other, never stopped believing in God or His plan. And I know they never will, even though Heaven parts them for the moment.

Thanks also goes to my cover designer, my editors, my publishers at Kindle Press, and to all the wonderful authors who joined my Kindle World and made First Street Church just as big a part of their hearts as it is mine. I cannot wait to read your contributions and to allow your words to touch my life as I know they will!

I must also thank my friend and Starbucks writing buddy, Mallory Crowe, for writing that one sentence when I needed help. It was a really good sentence, Mallory. Really!

Another person who helps get the words written in a major way? My fabulous, lifesaving assistant, Angi DeMonti. It's true! I'm only able to meet my writing deadlines by the grace of God and the persistence of Angi.

Lastly, a huge thank-you to you, the reader who embraced this story and read it through all the way to the end—and even read the acknowledgments, too. A gold star to you and a big, ol' hug.

My readers are incredibly special to me, and so many have become close friends. I need to tell you, Laurie Olsen, Rosemary Pfeiffer, Heidi Lynn, Jasmine Bryner, Jen Mello, Leona Ray, and countless others, you all make my life a happier place to live. Thank you, I love you, and I'll see you next time.

Sign up for even more free stories and uplifting messages from Melissa at www.MelStorm.com/gift.

The First Street Church Romances

Love's Prayer

Love's Promise

Love's Prophet

Love's Vow

Love's Trial

Love's Treasure

Love's Testament

Love's Redemption

Love's Resurrection

Love's Revelation

* * *

* * *

The Book Cellar Mysteries

Walker Texas Wife

Texas and Tiaras

Remember the Stilettos

Ladies, We Have a Problem

* * *

Stand-Alone Novels and Novellas

A Texas Kind of Love

A Cowboy Kind of Love

A Wedding Miracle

Finding Mr. Happily Ever After

A Colorful Life

My Love Will Find You

The Legend of My Love

Splinters of Her Heart

* * *

Melissa also writes children's books and nonfiction as
Emlyn Chand. Learn more about those works at
www.EmlynChand.com.

MORE FROM FIRST STREET CHURCH

READERS, FIND MORE BOOKS

Welcome to the tiny town of Sweet Grove, TX, where neighbors still care deeply about each other and the little white chapel on First Street is the heart and soul of all who live here.

It's a simple life–a good life–yet many here are suffering invisible pains. From alcoholism to divorce, hoarding, and even suicide, the struggles are real but so is the God who loves this town and all its residents. Through the darkest of times and the deepest of tragedies, each day provides a new chance to find faith, hope… and even love.

Our tiny town has grown by leaps and bounds,

thanks to the introduction of a new Kindle World. Many top Christian and Sweet Romance authors have already contributed their own stories to First Street Church, and many more are coming soon!

**Come see what's available at
www.sweetgrovebooks.com.**

* * *

Authors, contribute your story

Whose life will you change for the better? Will you bring new purpose to a troubled youth, redemption to a scorned elder, or perhaps salvation to the newest resident in town? Their fates and futures now rest in your capable hands.

www.sweetgrovebooks.com/authors

* * *

Everyone, join our community

Welcome to Sweet Grove, TX. We're so glad you came for a visit! Please don't be a stranger. Come join our wonderful community of Christian Romance readers on Facebook. Make sure to sign up for the Sweet Grove Sentinel to stay up-to-date with all the latest and greatest First Street Church news!

www.sweetgrovebooks.com/community

ABOUT THE AUTHOR

Melissa Storm is a mother first, and everything else second. She used to write under a pseudonym, but finally had the confidence to come out as herself to the world. Her fiction is highly personal and often based on true stories. Writing is Melissa's way of showing her daughter just how beautiful life can be when you pay attention to the everyday wonders that surround us.

Melissa loves books so much, she married fellow author Falcon Storm. Between the two of them, there are always plenty of imaginative, awe-inspiring stories to share. Melissa and Falcon also run the business Novel Publicity together, where she works as publisher, marketer, editor, and all-around business mogul. When she's not reading, writing, or child-rearing, Melissa spends time relaxing at home in the company of her three dogs and five parrots. She never misses an episode of *The Bachelor* or her nightly lavender-infused soak in the tub. Ahh, the simple luxuries that make life worth living.

Melissa loves hearing from readers.
Please feel free to reach out!

www.MelStorm.com
author@melstorm.com

96417295R00148

Made in the USA
Columbia, SC
26 May 2018